CHRYSALIDES

ALI COYLE

Improbable
PRESS

First published by Improbable Press in 2023

Improbable Press is an imprint of:
Clan Destine Press
www.clandestinepress.com.au
PO Box 121, Bittern Victoria 3918 Australia

National Library of Australia Cataloguing-In-Publication data:

Ali Coyle
Chrysalides

ISBN: 978-1-922904-07-2 (pb)
ISBN: 978-1-922904-08-9 (eb)

Cover artwork by © Willsin Rowe
Layout & Typesetting by Dimitra Stathopoulos

Improbable Press
improbablepress.com

I dedicate this book to every single person
who has ever read and commented on my fanfiction.

You gave me enough confidence in my writing
to submit stories without fear,
to weather rejections without despair,
and to acknowledge that 'writer'
is a core part of who I am.

CONTENTS

GOOD GENES

THERE WAS NO WARNING.

At the exact time to the second when Talulah Gordon – known as Tuli – turned eighteen-years-old, she looked at the collection of expensive gifts heaped at the foot of the unicorn-patterned duvet, hiccupped, retched, belched, and charred the lot with a jet of flame that started a few inches in front of her open mouth and ended a mere hair-width from the peach silk curtains of her bedroom.

Her mother, proud and pleased by her daughter's joy only seconds earlier, watched in horror as a few green-gold scales broke out on the skin of Tuli's precious forehead, the green in her hazel eyes seemed to glow, and her beautiful, soft, chestnut-brown hair hardened into a fearsome, glossy ridge. Then Tuli crashed back onto her pillow, fast asleep. She woke a couple of hours later complaining of a sore throat and asking for ice cream, unaware of the tumult she'd caused.

These *outbreaks*, as Tuli's parents referred to them in hushed tones the following weeks, were rarely so severe, but remained unpredictable. Tuli would go for days, almost two whole weeks once, without a single peridot scale pushing out from under her freckled skin. Some outbreaks were no more than a quick shimmer of color above Tuli's frowning, hazel eyes. Others had Tuli's father standing by with the garden hose, aching thumb pushing back against the water pressure at the open end, ready to douse any flames that licked up the furnishings while her mother corralled Tuli's younger brothers in their room and reminded them calmly of the family fire drill.

It could not, Lydia and Adam both agreed, go on. How could their darling troublesome teenager possibly return to school when an argument with a friend or a disagreement over homework could result in a charge of arson?

After heated discussions in hushed voices about how best to describe their pride and joy's affliction, doctors were carefully consulted in private. But all frowned and shook their heads and offered referrals to dermatologists and immunologists and psychologists. The sixth or seventh medical specialist Tuli's parents consulted typed something that looked, to Lydia's watchful eyes, like Munchausen-by-proxy. So, Lydia turned to the gaggle of alternative practitioners who hung around the fringes of modern medicine instead. She reluctantly discussed with Adam her misgivings about those *types* who mostly peddled half-mystical charlatanry to people with bank balances to match their desperation. Yet she felt that she had little choice.

Still baffled and running low on patience with a daughter who always slept through charring the bedspread every time she had so much as a bad dream, Tuli's parents turned to some definitely unconventional remedies. One practitioner, who called herself 'the country's most respected consultant cryptozoologist,' had a young assistant who frequently tried to interrupt with demands to meet Tuli, until the stern woman ran out of patience and snapped at her to be silent. The girl had looked to be only a little more than Tuli's age. Surely if she knew something it was because her boss had taught her, and the consultant insisted nothing could be done about a cure. However, after quizzing Mr and Mrs Gordon about their own parents and grandparents, she suggested that perhaps extensive genetic testing and professional genealogy might shed light on such a serious and inconvenient condition, but in the meantime perhaps the girl could be moved to a less flammable dwelling. With a flourish, she presented Tuli's parents with an eyebrow-raising estimate for scientific investigations with full board and lodging at her own private research center.

Lydia cursed at the news. Unwilling to throw good money after bad in the futile search for either medical or mystical advice, and even more unwilling to hand her daughter over to some opportunistic stranger, she and Adam gritted their teeth, tightened their belts, raided their savings, and put down the deposit for a stone-built cottage in one of the less-touristy parts of the Devon countryside, where the nearest neighbors were two miles away across the fields, and the broadband was good enough for Tuli to complete her education online.

She was to be home-schooled, of course. How, her mother asked her father, can we expect our little girl to cope with all the excitement and stresses of completing college while keeping her illness hidden? There were plenty of resources online that Tuli could use, and registering for exams was a problem for a future that, although only a few months away, felt very, very distant.

Adam flatly informed the family that he needed to be earning and he could not live away from his work. Tuli's twin brothers were happy in their primary school and wailed at the idea of leaving their friends behind. With her cheeks burning and her jaw set tight against anger and frustration, tears pricking at her eyelids, Lydia agreed that, for a little while anyway, maybe a few weeks, she would move with Tuli. She would get a job locally, get to know their new neighbors, and make the cottage nice for everyone. They would move when they were all ready.

But Lydia Gordon had underestimated the remoteness of their new home and overestimated her employment prospects as a middle-aged *offcomer* who *wouldn't last*. Although none of the pretty-voiced people who interviewed her for jobs said as much, there were locals in greater need of the modest, regular earnings on offer for work at the post office or village pub or supermarket in town fifteen miles away.

Lydia hated it. She hated the darkness of the night and the sense of insignificance she felt under the eyes of a million sprinkled stars. She hated the looming trees that stood in thick, dark silence punctuated by owl screeches that sounded like ghouls come to suck out her soul. Most of all, Lydia hated that she felt useless, unable to fulfil the promise she had made to her family, that she would make a life for them all here, and unable to fulfil her unspoken promise to Tuli that the family would be together again before she truly missed them.

Tuli, however, loved the countryside. She'd immediately adored the quirky little cottage that used to be a church schoolhouse, and still had the date chiseled above a front door that sat under a half-moon stained-glass window splashing blue and gold onto the tiles when the sunlight fell on it in the afternoon. She crowed about the big, oak door with the brass door knocker shaped like a wyvern and, at the far end of what would have been the schoolroom, a fireplace almost big enough swallow her, flanked by two inglenook seats.

Upstairs, she'd squealed with delight at the arc of the stained glass that peeped up into the modern bathroom, splashing a rainbow onto the floor where space for the upper storey had been created. The renovators had cleverly lowered the once-lofty ceiling of the schoolroom below and lifted the roof just high enough for her not to worry about banging her head. She especially loved that the front of the house looked into a forest of tall conifers in a million shades of green, trees shushing and swishing as they swayed in the breeze. She didn't mind at all that the back windows overlooked the overgrown graveyard and rectangular limestone outline of the church that had once stood there, before it was moved block by block to be restored in the village three miles up the twisting single-track road that wound its way past her home.

Lydia, having had no success in securing an income locally and suffering from a kind of blank loneliness she had not anticipated, was swayed by Tuli's father and brothers who missed her. They missed Tuli too, but weeks of nights with uninterrupted sleep – and the banishment of bad dreams featuring their house burning down – made them wary of asking her to come back.

"Please come home," Adam Gordon said to Lydia over the phone on the seventh Sunday afternoon. "I miss you. The boys miss you. It's been almost two months now. I know we've sheltered Tuli, but she's eighteen, and sensible. She's old enough to learn how to look after herself for a while. If she's studying her school lessons remotely then it doesn't matter whether she's here or there. We can pay her bills and order groceries to be delivered, and get the gas bottles changed and the heating oil tank filled up regularly. We'd only be a phone call and a car journey away. And surely a neighbor can look in, or we can get some cameras installed?"

Tuli sat at the top of the staircase and listened, her heart beating harder and her teeth worrying at her pink lips until the skin peeled and began to sting. "A neighbor." Lydia sighed. "It's not like the city, you know. There aren't any neighbors. Closest is the lady who runs the dairy farm and she's too busy."

Tuli closed her eyes tightly against the threatening tears and let her head sag sideways to bump the wall. Her mother was quiet for a few seconds, then spoke sharply. "Don't let's have this talk again. You know I've applied for every job going this side of the moors. And a few further away too."

Barely listening to her mother's words, only the tones in which they were spoken, Tuli imagined going back to her old home to stay with her noisy brothers and having to walk everywhere on pavements bordering roads that roared with honking, stinking cars. She imagined saying a too-brief goodbye to the forest and to the stories she made up for herself about the people whose headstones stood at jaunty angles behind the cottage, maybe having to pack that very night and leave in her mother's car for the long drive back to the city in the morning. That's what finally made her tears spill over. As she sobbed, she had no clue her skin broke out in rippling patterns of green and gold.

Gradually, Tuli became aware that her mother was standing halfway up the staircase, looking at her strangely. Her skin itched on her arms and on her legs under her jeans, and she rubbed flat palms over herself to calm the discomfort. "Are we leaving?"

Lydia blinked and smiled with a brightness that even Tuli could see was false, unshed tears sparkling her vivid green eyes, and shook her head. "No, darling girl. I still might get one of those jobs in the big town across the moor."

Tuli refused to meet her mother's gaze. "But you hate living here."

Lydia climbed the rest of the way up to sit beside her daughter. "You don't hate living here, do you?"

"I love it here." Tuli set her elbows on her knees and her chin in her hands. "I want to stay and not go back but if we have to we–" Tuli stopped and scrubbed her face with her sleeves, hiding her eyes.

Lydia put her arms around Tuli. "I think I need to go home. At least for a while. You know dad, he's probably feeding the boys cheese on toast or pizza every night. But if you really like it here, how would you feel about staying on your own for a little bit? Would you be very lonely?" Lydia sighed and spoke faster, quietly, as if to herself. "Of course you would be too lonely. What am I thinking? I can't leave you here. It wouldn't be fair on you to–"

Tuli's excitement surged as she understood what her mother was saying. She grabbed Lydia's arm, still wrapped around her, and pulled it and shook it and patted it. "Mum! I'll stay. I want to stay. Please, let me stay. I'll be fine on my own. I promise. I can cook and the village isn't that far away really and–"

Lydia's eyebrows shot up. "Talulah, are you sure? You won't…" She frowned uncertainly. "You won't set the place on fire or anything? By accident?"

Half in mirth and half in indignation, Tuli burst out laughing. "Mu-u-um, don't be daft. How on Earth would I do that? The whole place is made of stone." Lydia took a deep breath and hugged Tuli again. This time, Tuli leaned sideways against her mother and rested her head on Lydia's shoulder. "I'll phone dad and tell him myself. Will he be okay with me staying here by myself?"

Lydia chose her words carefully, rehearsed them in her head before speaking. "He misses you, and so do Jack and Jamie, but they'll understand that if you like it here and you want to stay, it doesn't mean you love them any less."

"Well." Tuli held out her hand. "Can I use your phone? Mine's charging."

Lydia stayed a few more days, long enough to fill the kitchen cupboards, set up deliveries of heating oil for the boiler and gas bottles for the cooker, buy and fit cameras to cover the front and back doors (Tuli flatly refused to be spied on indoors), and advertise in the post office window and in the local newspaper for a companion for Tuli. She arranged interviews of the three best applicants, one after the other, and scrubbed the kitchen table clean. Tuli was strictly instructed to wait upstairs until called to meet any candidate who passed Lydia's interrogation.

The first applicant, a woman in her thirties who brought along two small children, seemed lovely until the conversation moved on to the difficulties faced by new people moving into the area revealed some deeply held, extremely questionable beliefs. Tuli sat at her perch on the top stair with her hand over her mouth as Lydia politely escorted her to the door with a promise to phone her later.

The second applicant, a retired nurse with a delightfully jolly voice, seemed confused as to Tuli's age and kept asking if 'the old dear' needed any particular medical or physical assistance. Lydia ushered him out and closed the door with a promise to let him know as soon as she had made a decision. Lydia looked up at Tuli's perch. They locked eyes for a moment and both shook their heads slowly.

The time for the third applicant to arrive came and went. Lydia glared at her watch, but Tuli reminded her that the bus service ran to its own special timetable.

"That's all very well," Lydia said with an exasperated sigh. "But I really wanted someone with their own transport. What if there was an emergency?" As the words left Lydia's lips, a roar blossomed outside and cut off suddenly. Tuli scrambled upstairs to look out the window. Below, a petite figure stood on the gravel drive beside a dirt bike, took off a scuffed red helmet and shook out long, black hair before twisting her tresses up again in a scarf.

Tuli almost squealed. "Is that her? I like this one, mum. Mum? Mum!"

"She's on a motorbike! Tuli, you are absolutely not getting on a motorbike."

"No, but—"

Lydia put on her best stern voice. "Shush now. Wait up there."

Tuli scurried back to her favorite stair, ears alert for the new visitor, hoping she was nice and sensible and down-to-earth like her mum wanted, but also imagining she might be everything she herself wanted too. By the time Lydia had the door opened, the girl's leather jacket and helmet safely stashed in the under-stair cupboard, Tuli was already roaring along the single-track roads in her imagination, wind whistling past her and arms around the waist of the dark-haired girl riding up front.

Tuli shook the daydream away so she could concentrate on her eavesdropping. "I'm so sorry I'm a bit late," the girl was saying. "I had to stop and wait for the cows."

"The cows?"

"Yes. As I got to your turning there was a herd of cows coming down the road. Well. They weren't going to back up or stand aside for me, so I had to get out of their way. Nearly ended up in the ditch."

"Goodness! Are you okay?"

"Sure! Sure. It's normal around here. Best not to be on the farm roads at milking time."

"Do you ride your bike into ditches a lot, then?"

Tuli heard the girl laugh and imagined her hair flicking around as her head shook. "I'm very careful with it. That bike is my freedom. I need it to get to college on the other side of the moor."

"You're in college." Tuli could hear disappointment in her mother's dulled voice. "Won't that mean you'll be too busy for this job?"

"Not at all, Mrs Gordon. I pass your turning twice a day. I thought I could come in on my way to college to say good morning, then come back after my classes and maybe your daughter would like it if we had dinner and studied together."

The mental image of sitting across the kitchen table with frozen pizza to eat with their fingers and their schoolwork spread around, talking about their days and maybe watching TV after if there was time, was too much for Tuli to resist. She thundered downstairs, calling out, "Hi! Hi, I'm Talulah but you can call me Tuli. What's your name?"

The girl stood up from her chair at the kitchen table, a polite smile ready on her face. Her grin widened and her eyes sparkled when she saw Tuli's bubbling enthusiasm. "I'm Rishona Tremethyk. Nice to meet you, Tuli." Rishona's face relaxed into a smile as warm as the afternoon sunshine.

"Rishona! What a lovely name." Tuli stuck her hand out. "Does it mean something nice? It should."

Rishona was halfway through a shrug when she froze at the sight of a ripple of rosy-golden scales on Tuli's cheeks. She blinked away her stare and glanced at Lydia. Lydia held her breath, waiting for a question, or a yell, or for the girl to point and scream and run away. But Rishona blinked again and recovered her smile. "Tuli is a nice name too."

"Thank you!" Tuli's grin racked up another notch and this time the flurry of scales moved like a wave down her neck too. Just for a second. "Mum, can Rishona have the job?"

Lydia frowned. "I'm not sure. We need to have a talk and then we can make a decision together, sweetheart. Why don't you go for a walk in the forest for half an hour?"

"Oh, there are deer!" Rishona's face lit up. "Have you seen any yet?"

Although aware that she was being dismissed, the sting was

lessened by the thought that she might see deer and take a good photo to show Rishona later. Within three minutes, Tuli was out of the house with her coat half-on and her phone in her hand.

"So, Miss Tremethyk," Lydia said with a sigh. "You saw that my Tuli is a little different. I will understand if you would rather not take the position. You're a bit younger than I hoped for anyway." She directed a stern glare at Rishona. "I expect you to say nothing about Tuli's illness. Not to Tuli, not to anyone. She loves it here. I do not want to have to take her away."

"I've heard of Tuli before and I've met you, although you don't remember me," Rishona said with a serious shake of her head. "I was with my grandmother. We came to your house in the city, but she couldn't do anything. I wanted to ask so many questions, but she sent me out."

Lydia frowned deeper as she searched her memory. "We had so many people see her. Experts and…others. There seems to be no cure for her condition."

"Doesn't she know?" Rishona pushed her lukewarm tea mug around the table with her fingers. Lydia snatched it up and rinsed it in the sink.

"She knows there's something different about her. But she doesn't always notice her outbreaks, and often she forgets about them very soon afterwards. It only happens when she's excited or upset. So she needs to be kept calm. And secret. Safe." Lydia gave Rishona a meaningful look. "I need her to be safe."

"Tuli is not in any danger, Mrs Gordon. Not from me, anyway." Rishona met Lydia's serious gaze. "And I won't tell a soul. Look, I'm almost twenty. I'm old enough to be looking after myself and looking out for Tuli, I have transport and I have time and I really want this job. I brought my college reference, the one my teachers wrote to get me on my course. Do you want to see it?"

Lydia tightened her lips into a line. "What if Tuli gets hurt and you have to take her to hospital? You can't do that on your deathtrap."

Rishona raised her eyebrows, taken aback. She pulled her phone out of her pocket and held it up. "You get pretty decent signal here, so I'd call an ambulance. They'd probably send the helicopter."

Lydia still was not convinced of Rishona's suitability but there was nothing more to say so she sent the girl away with a promise to call later. She stood behind the closed door for almost a full minute, feeling the silence of the house around her, breaking it with a deep sigh before it settled too heavily on her shoulders. Perhaps it would be best if they both went back to the city after all. Tuli, having not gone too far into the forest, came running back, summoned by the cough of the dirt bike engine before it roared off along the road. She burst into the kitchen, looking all around her. "When does Rishona start? Tomorrow?"

Lydia closed her eyes for a second or two then shook her head. "No. She's not the right person for the job. She's too young."

Green and gold scales skittered up and down Tuli's bare arms and her eyes sparkled with amber flecks when the waves of scales washed over her face, reaching as high as her hairline and fusing her soft, wavy hair, just for an instant, into solid ridges. "But she's perfect!" Tuli wailed, a warning shimmer of heat around her lips. "She's exactly the right age. She's old enough to be like a sensible big sister to me. And I like her."

"But Talulah," Lydia said, taking a couple of steps backwards, "I can't be sure that she's reliable. I can't leave you here and not know you'll be safe. We need to sit down and discuss this calmly."

"You already decided without me!" Tuli huffed and wisps of smoke curled around her nostrils and drifted up to the ceiling. Her voice lowered in pitch and rose in volume. "That's not a discussion! That's you telling me how it is and expecting me to agree with you. Well, I don't! I'm not going back to our old house. I'm eighteen. I can look after myself."

"Tuli! We do not shout. Is that clear?" Lydia took one more step backwards. "Go to your room, calm down, and we will talk like adults after dinner."

"No!" Tuli's voice roughened to a rumble then she threw her

head back, let out a sound that began as a scream and ended as a deep roar, and blasted a jet of orange-tinged, blue flame that scorched an oval of paint off the ceiling.

Even before the flame died, Tuli fell to the floor, out cold. Lydia stared in horror for a few seconds before remembering this was her little darling, and running over to check Tuli's breathing and roll her onto her side. As she held her daughter's hand and waited for her to come round, she fetched her phone out of her pocket and sent a text message, then watched the screen as if that might make the reply flash up more quickly.

Tuli coughed and retched and groaned. "Sweetheart don't worry, you fainted. That's all." Lydia watched Tuli's eyelids flutter and open, hazel eyes devoid of amber set in pale, freckle-dusted skin with no sign of scales. She petted Tuli's soft, wavy hair and smiled. "How do you feel?"

"My head." Tuli stopped to cough again, voice gravelly and strained. "My head hurts. And my throat."

"I'll help you sit up then get you some water."

"Mm-hmm."

Lydia pulled and Tuli pushed and soon the girl was sitting on the floor with her back against the cabinets and her legs making a vee in front of her. She sipped then gulped the glass of tap-water Lydia offered her.

"Did I trip and fall? I ran back when I heard the bike. Or did I…" Tuli looked up at the blackened oval on the ceiling, but pretended not to see it. "So when does Rishona start?"

Lydia glanced at her phone and nodded her head once, a tight smile on her face. "Tomorrow."

Lydia remained at the cottage with her daughter for another week – just long enough to get to know her employee a little and to check Rishona's references with a couple of phone calls to the college and to her previous employer at the fish and chip shop two villages over. Rishona called in at the cottage at seven thirty every morning to spend fifteen minutes having polite coffee with Lydia and to laugh at Tuli's bed-hair. She called back on her way home at five thirty and cooked dinner, even enticing Tuli to help make Bolognese sauce, although persuading her to wash up afterwards was more of a challenge.

When Rishona revealed that she was studying biology and genetics at college and had to take additional courses in chemistry and mathematics, Tuli's face lit up with an excited smile and she begged Rishona to tutor her too, if Lydia would pay her extra for it. "I can't ask the online tutor in the videos any questions," Tuli pointed out to her mother after Rishona had gone home. "But Rishona would be right here so she could answer anything I need to know." And with only a brief frown as a token show of reluctance, Lydia agreed to pay for one more hour per week.

When it came time for Lydia to get into her practical little car and drive back to the city, both mother and daughter disguised their excitement about the imminent change in their lifestyles, using brittle humor to deflect their feelings and tamp down the guilt they each felt at looking forward to being away from one another after so much time together.

"I'll wait a bit," Lydia announced after closing the hatchback on her suitcase and checking her pockets for phone and wallet and keys. "I'll wait until Rishona arrives. In case you get upset."

"Mum, I'm eighteen, not eight." Tuli hugged her parent. "I promise I'll be fine." After a moment, when Lydia hadn't released her yet, Tuli added, "Will you?"

Lydia laughed and sniffled, held Tuli a little tighter. "Of course. I just worry about you, same as I worry about the boys and your dad." Tuli patted Lydia's back and stiffened up just enough to signal that she'd had enough. Lydia stepped back and wiped her eyes, presenting a watery smile. "I'll be back in a couple of weeks. Phone me if you need anything, okay? Even if it's just a bad dream and it's three in the morning, or if you want me to add ice cream to the grocery order, or if you need—"

"I can phone you at three in the morning for ice cream?" Tuli laughed. "Mum, I'll be fine."

To Tuli's relief, Lydia ruffled her hair, patted her cheek, told her not to dare call at 3am for ice cream, got into her car and drove away up the lane with her hand waving out of the window until she reached the corner.

Tuli did an excited little bounce and let out a whoop of delight. She felt like she was properly alone for the first time ever, and she supposed she must be a real adult now that she was responsible for her own routines and her own house and her own entertainment.

Back inside the kitchen, the cottage felt bigger. Her footsteps echoed on the tiled floor and when she asked the cream-colored, unevenly plastered walls aloud, "So, what do I want to do now?" her voice sounded odd, echoey, different to the voice that spoke to her inside her head whenever she thought about things. Louder, and with the memory of the words hanging in the air as if waiting for an answer.

The first thing Tuli did was put on some music and walk through the whole cottage, inspecting every room, looking inside every cupboard and drawer and peering under every bed. Satisfied that she found nothing other than the sweet, floral scent of her mother's toiletries in the little shower and some jeans and shirts of Lydia's folded neatly in a drawer, she ended her inspection downstairs at the fridge door.

Tightening her lips and puffing a breath out through her nose, she pulled the fridge open, breathed in the cooler air, and took stock of her supplies. She took out the cheese, looked around out of habit, broke off a crumbly corner of the perfect rectangle with her fingers, popped it into her mouth and laughed in pleasure at the taste of the illicit snack. A second corner succumbed to the same fate, then Tuli put the block back on the shelf and closed the door.

She was half-watching a nature documentary when Rishona clattered through the door and yelled out a greeting. Tuli was already on her feet, a grin chasing the boredom from her face, as Rishona put her helmet down and unpacked her laptop on the kitchen table. "Your mum said I was to ask you if you wanted me to stay over tonight. If that was okay with me. Which it is. I have homework too so we could study together."

Tuli's delight at having Rishona's company was marred by the implication that, in her mother's eyes at least, she was not old enough to be left alone overnight. "I don't need a babysitter," Tuli snapped with a scowl, then immediately shook her head and looked at Rishona with remorse. "Sorry. I mean, thanks but I'll be okay. You don't have to go to the trouble."

Rishona raised her eyebrows at Tuli's brief flash of temper but nodded in acceptance of her apology. "It's not any trouble. If you get lonely, I can stay over. Just let me know so that I can bring my things." She smiled and leaned a little closer. "You know, it might be fun."

Tuli shook her head again. When she spoke next it was with a large pinch of petulance. "I don't know why she doesn't trust me. Other people my age go off to college all the time and live away from their parents. It's not a big deal."

Rishona hung her leather jacket over the back of a kitchen chair and sat down. "Maybe she misses you. Maybe she feels guilty about leaving you and asking me to stay makes her feel better. Maybe this is hard for her too."

Tuli snorted in disgust and took the chair beside Rishona's, admiring the shiny, red dome of her crash helmet. "She's got dad and my brothers to fill my place."

Rishona shrugged. "You can't have it both ways. You can't say you want to be trusted to live on your own and complain about your mum leaving you at the same time."

"Watch me," Tuli said with a deep sigh. Rishona laughed quietly and, after a minute, looking up into Rishona's deep brown eyes, so did Tuli.

Tuli looked at her online science homework and asked Rishona a few questions about cell biology while Rishona made baked potatoes in the microwave. They ate together in silence at the kitchen table with laptops shoved out of the way and, to Tuli's dismay, Rishona suggested that Tuli do the washing up immediately instead of leaving their dishes in the sink as an irritation to be added to the next day. Rishona offered again to stay, but in her annoyance at having to do chores, Tuli insisted she was old enough to spend her first night without her mother alone. Rishona merely shrugged and smiled, packed away her things, put on her leather jacket and helmet and puttered away on her bike into the fading evening with a wave to Tuli, watching covertly from behind the curtain in Lydia's room.

It was her first night of freedom and Tuli intended to make the most of it. With no one to order her into bed at ten and nag her at five past that she'd be tired tomorrow, she'd stay up all night if she wanted. She put on her PJs and chose a movie to stream, one that her mother would forbid on account of the risk of nightmares. Then she made a pot of tea all for herself and settled on the sofa. The film she selected was horror and, she realized as it ended and the house was lit only by the eerie glow of the TV screen, a mistake. She felt like every hair on her bare forearms and the back of her neck was standing on end, and the normal creaking and cracking sounds of an old house settling in the night chill took on ominous significance to her heightened senses.

The oil-fired boiler in the kitchen clicked and hissed. Water gurgled in the radiator. Tuli shot to her feet, leapt across the room and flicked the lights on. Blinking in the bright glare, she laughed at herself. Walking through to the kitchen with her empty mug, putting the kettle on to boil again, she decided on another film to calm her nerves. Something she could laugh at and maybe sing along to. While waiting for the kettle to boil, she darted around the house, closed all the curtains and put a light on in every room.

She returned to the sofa and the television to find that the broadband had cut out. A short investigation of the settings revealed her worst fear: her mother had set up an internet curfew from eleven at night until six in the morning and she did not have the password to remove it. She grabbed her phone intending to text her mother and demand the password, but she wasn't so furious that she couldn't think straight. She forced herself to put her phone down before she sent a text in anger and revealed that maybe she did need the curfew, but she yelled in frustration at the blank screen. An unexpected shift in color caught Tuli's attention. She frowned, distracted by the swirling patterns of green and gold and red under the skin on the backs of her hands. She shrieked when inch-long, curved, golden talons erupted from her nail beds, throwing her arms out in front of her as if to get her hands as far away from herself as possible. She turned her head to look for her phone, saw her left hand make a futile, panicked scrabble to get hold of it, then blacked out on the sofa as her phone hit the carpet.

The next thing she knew, she was cold, stiff, and had a gloved hand roughly shaking her shoulder. "Oh, it lives! Look at the state of your PJs." Rishona said, a little more sarcastic and a little louder than necessary.

Tuli blinked and sat up. "Shit. I was watching a film. Must have fallen asleep." She stretched and shook out her arms, frowning at the torn seams and stretched fabric. "Ugh, these were my favorite. Guess they fell apart from being worn so much. But I had a cool dream that I had claws and scales."

Turning to watch Rishona, Tuli raised her eyebrows, waiting for the older girl's response. Rishona shifted her grip on her helmet. She opened her mouth as if to say something, but sucked her teeth instead, put on a bright smile. "Was it a creature feature? I love those. Especially if the special effects are a bit rubbery." Her face turned serious. "Tuli, you left the back door wide open last night. I know people talk about times past when you could leave your doors open and nobody would bother, but that's because nobody had anything worth stealing. You need to be more careful."

"I locked up!" Tuli glared at Rishona then her face fell into an uncertain frown. "At least I'm pretty sure I remember locking the door."

"Well, you better double check in future." Rishona reached out and picked a fleck of something out of Tuli's hair. "Gracie up at the shop said she saw something on fire in the forest when she got up in the night. She called the emergency services, but it was gone when she looked again so she called them back to say don't bother coming out." She waited while Tuli got to her feet, groaned and stretched and padded to the kitchen and put the kettle on. "I'll see you later. You need anything?"

Tuli yawned and shook her head. "No. Thanks. Oh, could you ask my mum for the internet password?"

Rishona laughed. "I can ask but don't get too hopeful. Here." She held her hand over the worktop beside Tuli and dropped the fleck she had picked out of Tuli's hair, then put on her helmet and left.

Tuli frowned at the fragment of pinecone, one edge thick and brown, the other blackened and leaving a gray-brown smear on her skin when she rubbed it. Then the kettle clicked off and she flicked the charred fragment into the bin because ignoring the issue for now was much easier then facing it, and set about making some toast.

But as she finished her breakfast, Tuli remembered the charred fragment of pinecone. She plucked it back out of the bin and examined it, noting the way the blackened side marked her skin. She held it to her nose and closed her eyes, and a vague feeling of familiarity settled on her. It wasn't quite a memory, there was not nearly enough detail for that, but she knew something had happened last night. Something important she couldn't quite pin down.

Had she gone outside during the night, she wondered as she dumped her plate and mug into the sink for later. Was there more to the agreed story that her stress-induced illness caused an unusual skin condition and occasional burst of heat? She stared into the sink then ran the hot tap, concentrating on the simple task of rinsing her dishes to put off calling her mother and telling her a tale of maybe having gone sleepwalking right out of the house in the middle of the night.

Tuli shook her head and huffed out a laugh, blinking back tears as she set her plate on the draining board. Maybe she had gone out and forgotten about it, but there was no need to call. After all, Tuli reassured herself, if she had gone sleepwalking, she'd come to no harm. And if she hadn't gone out then there was no need to worry Lydia with her fears.

At least Rishona didn't know about her illness. Tuli reassured herself of this as she logged in to her online learning program. She thought she couldn't bear it if Rishona was to see her skin break out in scales, and think she was ugly or weird.

A morning of online lessons about mathematics and chemistry drained Tuli's interest completely. She chatted by text between activities with her mother (yes, she'd eaten breakfast and yes, she was sticking to her study schedule, but of her vague plan to ask for motorcycle lessons for her 'early birthday' she said nothing). She chatted on and off with Rishona too, and Rishona suggested that Tuli use the afternoon daylight to practice art and catch up on biology later, so Tuli packed a flask of tea, sandwiches, and her smaller sketchpad and pencils into her backpack and set off into the forest. She darted back to the house two minutes later to make sure she had locked the door behind her.

As she trod the now-familiar track between the trees, Tuli felt the sense of peace and belonging that the forest always settled upon her. The breeze was not strong enough to do much more than sway the thinnest branches high above, and the silence was disturbed only by birdcalls (these she tried to copy so that she could remember and look them up later), and the occasional rustle from a sudden flurry of activity from some small creature in the leaf litter. She realized with a warm flush that she was looking out for deer so she'd have something to tell Rishona over dinner, maybe have a sketch of one for Rishona to smile at, anything to make the only slightly older but, in her eyes at least, far more grown-up girl pay attention. Maybe if she asked, Tuli mused as she chose a spot to sit, Rishona would stay for the evening and watch a movie with her.

While she sketched, Tuli imagined what film she might suggest.

It would have to be just the right one. Something Rishona would be desperate to see, perhaps another scary film so she could pretend to be brave, hold Rishona's hand if she jumped, or pretend to hide her face in Rishona's shoulder if Rishona was the brave one. She decided she should detour to get snacks at the village shop, so their fingers could touch in a shared bowl of popcorn and they could laugh about it. It was only a bit over an hour to walk there and back if she cut through the forest instead of using the road that wound around its edge. She could, Tuli decided, do with getting a motorbike of her own as soon as she was brave enough to apply for her license.

Engrossed in drawing and daydreaming, Tuli lost track of time and only realized she was late when she heard her name being called over and over from somewhere back towards the cottage. She swore, stuffed her things back into her bag, and set off at the fastest trot she could manage without tripping over roots or twisting her ankle in the uneven dips between the trees.

Rishona met her where the main path split. "I was worried," she snapped. "You should have left a note."

"I was fine," Tuli snapped back, but her defensive irritation collapsed at the sight of Rishona's genuine relief. "I was fine," she repeated more gently. "I went out to draw. I thought you'd know where I was. It was your idea. I'm sorry."

Rishona blew out a sigh and held her hands out to Tuli. Tuli accepted the invitation and stepped into a hug. Rishona released her after a few warm seconds. "I suppose that's fair," Rishona said, smiling. "Okay. I'll phone you if you're ever out when I arrive again. But leave a note anyway. I need to know you're okay."

Tuli followed Rishona back to the cottage and into the kitchen. She pulled out her sketchbook. "Want to see what I drew?"

Rishona looked up from the cupboard, holding two large potatoes, one in each hand. She studied Tuli's drawing of a dark-haired girl on a motorbike closely then stood back to take in the whole scene. Her smile sparkled and she laughed in delight, "That's really good! Is it me?" Tuli nodded and just for a moment she thought Rishona looked unsure of herself. Rishona put the potatoes down, wiped her hands and took the sketchbook from Tuli. "Can I keep it?"

Tuli nodded again and Rishona carefully detached the page before slipping it inside a textbook from her backpack.

"Thank you." Rishona held Tuli's gaze for long enough that Tuli's cheeks started to feel warmer. Tuli looked away, then looked back. Rishona was still looking at her, but looked down as if she'd been caught. Rishona picked up the potatoes again and handed them to Tuli. "Put the oven on. These'll be ready after your biology lesson tonight. What do you want me to teach you about?"

Tuli settled at the kitchen table with her laptop open at her online course schedule and pointed. "That," she said. "Genetic inheritance. I read that if my dad has blue eyes and my mum has green eyes then mine ought to be green or blue too, not sludgy brown. So either genetics is fake or I'm adopted."

Rishona peered into Tuli's eyes. Tuli held her breath and gazed back into Rishona's dark irises while her heart hammered so loud that Rishona must surely hear. "Your eyes are a lovely hazel color with amber that shifts in the light." Rishona said with a laugh. "Genetics is not fake, I promise. But they teach you a lot of dumbed-down stuff at school level. Want to know what's really going on with eye color? It's fascinating."

Rishona lectured as if she was telling a story, and Tuli listened, captivated more by the cadence of Rishona's voice than the subject matter. Sometimes Rishona stopped, repeated herself and tapped Tuli's notepad and Tuli wrote down what Rishona said was important. The kitchen gradually became warm from the oven and dark from the sunset, lit by a harsh glare from the laptop screen and a softer, yellowish glow from the glass door of the oven.

When Rishona's lecture ended, Tuli pushed away her laptop and got up to put the lights on. "I think my brain is full now."

"Look up some exam questions and do one while I finish making dinner. Cheese or beans?"

"Both, please."

"Okay." Rishona took a can of beans from another cupboard and the cheese from the fridge, raising her eyebrows at the nibbled-off corners. "If I'm making two toppings, you can do two questions."

Keen to impress, Tuli did as Rishona asked, but with half of her attention fixed on planning the right time to ask Rishona to stay. But as Rishona slid two plates onto the table and sat down, she looked at her phone and said she wouldn't have time to stay and help with the washing up. To make up for the disappointment of missing Rishona's company, Tuli researched motorcycle licenses, started the online application process, and ordered a crash helmet. That, she reasoned, gave her permission to imagine how it would feel to be flying along the little roads on Rishona's bike, with her arms clinging tightly around Rishona, leaning into her back, both of them laughing for the joy of it.

Tuli settled into a routine. She'd get up and shower before Rishona arrived, eat breakfast while Rishona gave her a rundown of the gossip from Gracie up at the village shop, then hug her goodbye and text her mother to say she was fine and tell her if she needed anything. Mornings were for lessons, afternoons were for walks and drawing and daydreaming. Evenings were for an inventory of her education over spaghetti or baked potatoes or frozen pizza with Rishona. Since Rishona never spoke down to her, Tuli found herself getting more comfortable with her rush of feelings towards the other girl.

Yet every time she thought she was brave enough to say, "do you want to stay and watch a movie with me?" a nasty little voice would whisper in her ear, *what if it all goes wrong? What if she laughs at you because you're still a school-kid and too young for her, and she leaves and quits and you never see her again?* And she would forget the sentences she'd rehearsed in her head and say nothing of her nascent desires.

She sat as close to Rishona at the kitchen table as she thought Rishona would allow, elbows and shoulders bumping, hands meeting on the laptop keyboard sometimes to the sound of laughing apologies. They shared one-pot stews, eating with spoons and forks from an oven dish set between them to save on the washing up. They shared stories, Tuli hanging on every word of village gossip that Rishona spilled, and Rishona smiling as Tuli rambled about what her parents and brothers had said on their latest video call. And when Tuli would steal a glance at Rishona and see that the older, wiser girl was looking at her too, they'd both laugh and look away.

At last, Tuli's mother announced she would be coming back because in three weeks' time she'd be starting a job as the events manager for a big hotel. It was in one of the seaside towns that, although not quite local, was close enough she could live in when she had shifts and come home when she had days off.

"I'll be away Thursday mornings until Monday evenings," Lydia said, beaming from Tuli's phone screen. "But I'll be home Monday, Tuesday and most Wednesday nights."

"That's brilliant, mum," Tuli replied, beaming a smile through the screen at Lydia. Taken aback by the strength of her emotion at the thought of seeing her mother regularly again, her eyes prickled. She'd expected she might feel resentment born out of the hurt she'd felt at being left, even though she'd begged to be allowed to stay alone. But her sheer relief that her mum was coming home made her blink back happy tears.

Lydia waited a moment for Tuli to absorb the news before she asked, "Sweetheart, do you still need Rishona to come over on the days I'm not there?"

Tuli huffed out a surprised, nervous laugh. Her heart clenched in panic at the thought of losing the friend she'd come to think of as a soulmate. "Yes, mum," she said with some force. "I still need Rishona."

Lydia frowned. Tuli considered for a few seconds what might persuade her mother that Rishona was essential. "She's a great tutor. She says she'll help me register at her college as an external candidate and she'll take me there to sit my exams."

"Oh!" Lydia's face cleared and her smile returned. "That's a good idea. I thought you would be able to go back to your old school for that, but they off-rolled you last week. I might have said some rude things about it to the head teacher."

The image of Lydia facing down pompous old Mr McAllister made Tuli hoot with joy. "I wish I'd seen that," she said with a wide grin. "I bet he thought you were a proper fire-breathing dragon."

Lydia's image froze for just long enough that Tuli asked if there was a connection problem, then she was back, all smiles. "I suppose Rishona has been very reliable. All right. I hope she doesn't plan on taking you to her college on the back of that death trap she rides around on."

After a cry of, "Mu-u-um!" Tuli laughed and Lydia pulled a face, then laughed too. They ended the call, and Tuli looked forward to telling Rishona the good news.

Rishona replied to Tuli's excitedly ungrammatical text with an immediate phone call. "Great news about you mum. Isn't it?"

"Yes. I didn't realize I missed her that much. You're still coming over, right? I mean, I'll still be on my own a lot."

"Yes!" Rishona laughed in relief. "I was worried that was it, you know? Thanks and bye-bye."

"No way!" Tuli held the phone tight to her ear. "We're friends too, aren't we?"

Rishona went quiet for a few seconds. Tuli could hear background noise. A swell of TV and a door closing, perhaps. "I'm really happy you said that we're friends. I'd really miss you if I had to stop coming over."

Tuli chewed her lip while wondering whether to say more. But she just laughed and replied, "I'd miss you too. Hey, maybe we could switch Monday and Tuesday evenings for an extended weekend visit?"

"We can go on ecology field trips," Rishona suggested. "I'd love to show you the forest properly or take you up onto the moor."

In case Tuli was not enamored of the thought of fresh air and exercise, Rishona sealed the deal with the promise that there would be ponies grazing between the tors.

The days compressed noticeably over the next couple of weeks as the nights pushed out their dawn and dusk boundaries. The dark greens and browns of the forest became the only relief from the gray skies, hoof-churned fields, and narrow farm roads where muddy, black and white cows trudged to and from milking twice a day. Tuli saved the best daylight hours for wrapping up warm and walking in the forest, carrot slices in one pocket and an apple or two in the other in case she met a deer. These offerings, she would leave here and there off the main paths, beside the little rabbit tracks that darted between the trees like the traces of lightning bolts. At places where the orange carrot rounds had vanished, she would leave more. At the places where they remained, apple chunks browned and softening, carrot dried up but still bright against the tufts of tired grass, she would kick them out of sight with a sigh.

Sometimes, Tuli came across rough circles or ovals scorched into the tussocky grass and fine, brown, needle-like leaf litter. Other people used her forest, she realized, and reminded herself with a huff that although the forest must belong to someone, there were no 'keep out' signs and no fences. It was open to everyone who wanted to run a zigzag route through the trees carrying map and compass, or let their dogs run free on the rough gravel tracks used by the trucks that sometimes came early and empty, and left late, piled high with felled trunks. She was so used to being comfortably alone in her forest that she had a sense that she was its guardian and nobody else ought to trespass. They certainly ought not to be lighting campfires that left such obvious stains on the forest floor and occasionally charred the trunks to well above head height.

A couple of times a week, Tuli ventured out through the far side of the forest and into the village to buy milk and snacks. Gracie, who owned the shop, did not often speak to her, beyond what was necessary for securing a sale. Sensing disinterest, Tuli did not usually try to chat. On a day where the chill air pinked her cheeks and made shifting shapes of Tuli's breath as she jogged through the forest and the trees wafted mist from their green tops, Gracie watched Tuli as she perused the chocolate display, milk carton in her left hand and her right hand hovering over the gaudy packaging. Tuli chose, and placed her items on the wooden countertop.

"You'll not be going back through the forest, will you now." Gracie's tone made her question sound like an assumed fact.

Tuli pulled a handful of coins from the pocket of her beige parka. "My leggings are already damp and it's the shortest way home." She added with a shrug, "Why wouldn't I?"

Gracie pursed her lips and watched Tuli count out the exact change. "It's not safe," she said eventually, scooping the cash from the countertop. "I hear things, and I'm not one for gossip, but twice now the lads from the deer stalk and a couple of other folks out after rabbit and venison," Gracie tapped her nose and gave Tuli a theatrical wink. "Well, they've said there's more than just Thumper and Bambi in that forest."

Tuli's skin prickled and her voice faltered. "What – what else is there?" she asked, stumbling over the words, tongue drying in her mouth.

Gracie shrugged. "I don't want to say in case you think I'm stupid for listening to a couple of idiots with shotguns and too much time on their hands. Just saying you don't want to be in the forest at dusk, that's all. Best stick to the road. You want a bag for that?"

Tuli shook her head and dropped her shopping into her backpack, then thanked Gracie politely, gave her a nervous smile and slipped out into the late afternoon air. It was far from dark, yet the day was waning and the sky felt low and heavy overhead, as if struggling to shoulder the weight of the gray clouds. Tuli fastened her coat and looked along the road to where the rough pavement merged into the grass verge as it rounded the corner leading her the long way home. She jumped back, heart pounding and head buzzing, as a car roared by. She huffed at herself and shook her head, then pulled up the faux fur trimmed hood and turned to go back into her forest.

She would, Tuli promised herself as she passed between the first rows of trees, keep her eyes open. Although the sun had probably already started to melt into the horizon somewhere beyond the clouds, it was still light enough for her to see her way and would be for a while. Night arrived early but crept in slowly. It was something to do with latitude and the atmosphere bending the last sunlight, according to her physics teacher back when she went to school in person, but although she had some understanding of the concepts, she could not have explained it to anyone else.

Tuli smiled and thought about how she might look it up and explain to Rishona why late autumn nights gently settled down over her forest instead of falling like lead from the darkening sky. Grinning widely at the near-black, pillar-like trunks, she imagined Rishona's rolled eyes and the impatient tap of her fingers on the table to get her attention back on her lessons. After playing at being the model student, this was a new game she had been trying out for a week or so. See if she could drift off topic and then get Rishona to talk more about herself. For despite the weeks and weeks of daily visits, Tuli knew only that Rishona was a college student, loved goat's cheese pizza, and guarded her independence.

Despite her daydreams, despite her heightened emotions due to the anticipation of Rishona's visit, and despite the darkness that slunk between the trees and made her wonder if perhaps the road would have been a more sensible route after all, Tuli did keep herself alert for anything different from the usual hoots and caws and screeches from the treetops. Here and there she had noticed more signs of fires. Some had thick, black, sooty trails licking up tree trunks and it made her angry all over again that people would be so careless.

She paused, putting down her bag to examine a patch of charred bark on a tall spruce tree. Although it had been almost fully dark, Tuli found now that she could see better than she expected, and she glanced up to check if there was a full moon looking through a break in the clouds, but the sky remained black and gray between the deep shadowed boughs overhead.

A crack made Tuli whirl around, staring in horror, fear creeping up her spine and over her skin, tightening in her throat. A figure in a camouflage jacket stared back, black eyes in a pale face, mouth open, hand raised and pointing at her. To her surprise, the man backed away, never shifting his gaze, feet picking up high to avoid stumbling over roots, his other hand sliding to a long, slim leather bag slung over his shoulder. Tuli realized almost too late what he was doing. Rooted to the spot, when she saw the stock of the shotgun emerge from its slip, she took the deepest breath she could and screamed.

She woke up with a start and yelled. Rishona's hands were on her shoulders. Reassuring but firm words penetrated her fear. "Lie down. Relax. You're okay."

Tuli blinked at the living room ceiling for a minute then frowned and sat up slowly. "I went out to get milk," she said. "I was coming back through the forest and…" She sighed. "And that's all. I had…oh!" Images flitted through her mind. "I just had the weirdest dream. I was in the forest and there was a man getting ready to shoot me and I screamed at him, but it wasn't just a scream, there was a roaring noise in my ears like waves crashing and then there were flames everywhere and he dropped his shotgun and ran away." Tuli met Rishona's steady gaze and laughed. "Sorry I must have come back, changed into clean clothes, and fallen asleep."

Rishona's face was unreadable. "Must have, if you say so," she said, then she sighed. "You start making dinner. Baked potatoes, okay? I need to make a phone call."

Tuli got up slowly when Rishona offered her both hands and helped ease her to her bare feet. She followed Rishona to the kitchen and opened the fridge, aware of the opening and closing of the back door that led from the kitchen to the rectangle of garden that separated the cottage from the forest, weedy vegetable beds and tired-looking grass spotted with copper and golden fallen leaves, slipping into winter dormancy.

Tuli took the two biggest potatoes from the vegetable drawer and carried them to the sink to scrub their skins of grit. Rishona was halfway down the garden, far enough that Tuli could hear her speaking but not so close that she could eavesdrop. The hiss and splash of water from the tap and the gurgle in the pipes drowned out Rishona's voice almost completely, even though Rishona had wandered closer to the house again and was gesturing animatedly as if whoever she was lecturing was actually there. Happy with her work after only a few seconds, Tuli shut off the water and picked up a fork to prick the skins like Rishona had shown her.

Her hands stilled as some of Rishona's words reached her.

"She is, gran, I know it. No, she's completely unaware of her transformations. At least she hasn't mentioned them to me. She has blackouts when it happens and wakes up later with funny dreams. I found her half-naked in the forest this time. Well, I didn't think so either! But she's almost roasted the poachers three times now. I don't care if they deserved it, Tuli's in danger. What if someone actually believes them next time they're down the pub telling everyone who'll listen about how a dragon lives in the forest? They'd be…oh." Rishona's hand fell away from her face, phone display a bright rectangle in the black night. She stared at Tuli, standing between her and the open back door, potato in one hand and fork in the other. "Got to go, gran," Rishona said, eyes locked on Tuli's. "I'll call you later."

Tuli watched Rishona click her phone off and slide it into her pocket. Her skin prickled and her head swam but her vision and hearing sharpened. She could make out the lines of the tree trunks that moments ago had merged into soft shadows, and she somehow knew that the faint rustling from the branches was a soft-feathered tawny owl ruffling its wings and looking out for unwary nocturnal voles and mice. Tuli's limbs felt coiled tight, ready to spring this way or that, and a frisson ran down her back, across her shoulders and up through her hair, making every tiny muscle tingle on her scalp. She blinked. "What were you taking about," she wanted to ask. But words didn't come.

"Tuli," Rishona said, hands out and palms down as if balancing or trying to find her way in the dark. "Tuli, it's okay. You're okay. Don't panic."

Tuli could smell Rishona's herbal shampoo, a fresh note under the familiar, sweet and warm scent of her sweat. There was another odor too, one like the sharpness she remembered now from the man with the shotgun. Is that what fear smells like? Tuli wondered, eyes still locked with Rishona's, not daring to move. Rishona's wary motions gave away that she was nervous, but she hadn't tried to attack or to run. Tuli stood still, hands out as if offering the potato and fork to Rishona, who repeated over and over the same words of reassurance that Tuli was safe. She risked a glance at her hands. The potato and fork fell, forgotten, to the ground. She lifted her arms higher to examine with alarm the pattern of green and golden scales that covered her palms and the backs of her hands and the strong, curved talons that tapered where her blunt and bitten fingernails ought to be, from a thickened cuticle base to treacherous looking points.

"Tuli, you're still in there. You're still you," Rishona said, somewhere between an instruction and a question. "Aren't you? You're controlling this. You can change back whenever you want. Can't you?"

Tuli turned her attention back to Rishona. She saw the uncertainty in her friend's expression and she felt her own anger grow. Something was happening to her and Rishona knew more than she was letting on and hadn't told her. Rishona had lied by hiding the truth from her. Rishona was not her friend. She was spying on her, reporting on her to someone else and–

Tuli raised her head and dropped her hands, feeling tightness in her back and chest where her shirt was stretched to its limit by leathery webbing that started at her wrists and strained against the soft confines of ring-spun cotton. Her balance altered as her center of mass lowered, muscles thickening in her thighs and tendons pulling her forwards and down into a crouch, The discomfort fueled her anger. She tore at the fabric, talons ripping through the t-shirt and dropping it as rags on the ground. She shook herself and stretched out her wings, flapping them with strong, slow sweeps that didn't quite lift her from the ground but promised they could, if that was what she desired. She could fly and burn and then Rishona would wish she had told the truth – all of it – and…

And this time she knew she would remember. Tuli glared at Rishona. Rishona seemed so small, crouched as if ready to spring away and run. Tuli took a deep breath and arched her back, feeling air cool in her chest and something hot in her throat, something that had to come out or she'd explode from the effort of keeping it contained. She felt powerful in finally knowing what she was now, experiencing a dizzying sense of rightness at her full transformation. She turned a little away from Rishona, who hugged her arms around her knees and had her leather jacket pulled up over her head, and let out a single, long jet of blue flame tinged with yellow and orange, then swayed on her clawed feet as her center of mass shifted up and back again, and sat down heavily on the ground. Rishona uncurled and leapt over to Tuli, cradling her head and patting her cheeks.

"Come on," Rishona said with a relieved little laugh that ended with a swallowed sob. "Let's get you inside and see if we can sort this mess out."

Tuli managed the walk, head spinning and senses reeling from all the sounds of the forest. Her heightened senses told her there were people, two of them, prowling between the trees, too far away to see or hear her, but she shrank into Rishona's side anyway. Rishona's arm supported her around her back and a constant stream of calm, kind words grounded her. Rishona guided Tuli to a kitchen chair and she sat, leaning both arms on the table, holding on as if afraid she might slither off.

"Who were you talking to? About me. You were talking about me. On the phone."

Rishona sat at the chair around the corner of the table and took Tuli's left hand in both of hers. She turned it this way and that, smoothing the skin with firm strokes from wrist to fingertips. Tuli shivered at the touch.

"My grandmother," Rishona replied. "She's a cryptozoologist. We've known about you for a while. Gran and I came to London to see if we could help. Do you remember that? It was early last year. I'd just started working with gran. I was so excited to have the chance to meet a real shapeshifter that I talked too much and gran sent me to wait outside."

Tuli frowned, pulled her hand back and rubbed her head, her fingers separating the clumped ridge of chestnut hair into strands. "There were so many doctors. I always thought it was because of the blackouts." She rubbed her face, stretched her arms and rolled her shoulders. "I got fed up with being prodded and having blood tests done and having mum and dad talking to strangers about me as if I wasn't there." She shook out her arms and rubbed her neck, then crossed her arms over her bare torso. Her voice turned harsh. "So you've been spying on me this whole time? Did my mum and your gran plan this?"

"It's not like that." Rishona sat back. "I promise. I didn't know it was you when I applied for the job. Not until—"

A rash of copper ran along Tuli's arms. She smoothed the scales down from elbow to wrist and glared at Rishona. "I thought you were my friend but you're not, are you?" Tuli's shoulders curved and her neck elongated. Her hair seemed to shift under its own power to thicken into a ridge that ran from forehead to nape. Her voice roughened. "I thought there was something wrong with me. You knew all along and you never told me. You're a liar."

Eyes glistening, Rishona grabbed Tuli's hands and held on tightly. "I never lied to you, Tuli. I wanted to tell you but you never remembered. All those times you changed, you forgot or you thought it was a dream. I didn't see the point in saying anything. I thought you wouldn't believe me, or you'd think I was making fun of you. Tuli, I promise I am your friend."

Tuli's glare came through bright amber eyes with black slitted pupils, a fine dusting of gold on her lids that only resolved into scales when Rishona leaned closer. "I promise, Tuli. I never meant to hide anything from you. I was going to tell you. When the time was right." She huffed out a little laugh. "I suppose this is it, then. There just isn't a right time."

Tuli regarded Rishona's face as coolly as she could. She could feel emotions churning inside her – anger and hurt and betrayal – and she desperately wanted to run from the cottage, from Rishona, into the forest and give devastating vent to her feelings with no regard for who else might see her fire or hear her roar. She jerked her hands back from Rishona's grip and flexed her fingers, nails already thickening and tapering again. "So?" she snapped. "What were you telling your gran about me? I remember her now. She was the one who wanted to keep me in her lab, wasn't she? I bet you've been telling her all about me so that she can come and get me for her research. That's what she wanted, isn't it?"

Rishona sat back and sighed, staring at the table surface where Tuli's talons had gouged a short set of parallel lines when she had closed her hands and scraped the wood. Tuli growled deep in her throat. "Isn't it!" she demanded when Rishona, eyes closed tightly and face reddening, showed no inclination to answer. "I'm right, aren't I?"

"No!" Rishona lurched forward suddenly, her own anger and frustration overruling her disciplined calm and making her voice rise in volume as she spoke. "You're so wrong. Yes, gran wants you to live in her lab and yes she wants to study you, but I am not spying on you for her and I am not reporting to her about you. That was the first time I have said anything to her at all! And do you want to know why?" Rishona thumped the table with both fists, making Tuli flinch. "Because I was scared, Tuli. Fucking terrified! Of what might have happened to you out there. I came here and found you missing, and I went into the forest and it is so lucky that I found you first and brought you home."

Tuli stared, anger and fear turning to alarmed surprise at the force of Rishona's response. "My grandmother is not the only person interested in shapeshifters like you. If word gets out that there's a fucking dragon living alone in the middle of nowhere, you'll be captured and taken away and if you're lucky maybe you end up in someone's private collection where you're fed every day and brought out to light the barbecue at the weekends. Or maybe you end up being made to fight against a minotaur or a werewolf or a gorgon while some rich shitbag gathers bets on you. Tuli, I can't let that happen to you. I thought you were safe, hiding here on your own. But if you're out of control, rampaging around the forest, you're a danger to yourself." Rishona took a steadying breath, then added, "And others. You could hurt someone. What about that poacher? Out after deer? What if he'd been closer?"

Tuli's fury extinguished as if doused in ice-water the instant she understood what Rishona had avoided saying. "I could have hurt you," she said, voice small, sitting back, feeling the tingle in her fingers and toes as talons shrank and flattened into fingernails and toenails. Her skin itched all over and she rubbed her palms over her bare arms and shoulders, ending with her arms hiding her bare chest again. Rishona got up and slung her leather jacket over Tuli's shoulders. Tuli snuggled into its warmth and pulled it closed. "I wouldn't have. I promise. I wouldn't have hurt you. I wouldn't ever."

"I wasn't so sure about that." Rishona shivered. "I thought you were going to burn me up but you aimed away at the last second."

"I wouldn't. I couldn't ever do that. I'm sorry I scared you." Tuli stared morosely at the damaged tabletop. "I'll understand if you hate me and want to quit. Mum can probably find me another babysitter."

Rishona laughed quietly and got up. "I don't hate you and I'm not your babysitter, Tuli. I'm your friend." She paused to look at Tuli for a long moment. Tuli looked up eventually and Rishona smiled. "Maybe we can have pizza. I think potatoes will take too long now."

Tuli nodded and got up. She called over her shoulder on her way to the stairs. "I'll get a shirt."

"Tuli?" Rishona looked away when Tuli stopped and turned. "Do you mind if I stay the night?"

Tuli's heart thumped so hard in her chest and her head felt so light that she thought she might have to sit down. "I'd like that," she replied, turning away to hide her warming cheeks. "Mum's room's just sitting there empty, or we could share mine. You can pick a film if you want."

Rishona's call of "Thanks!" reached Tuli when she was already halfway up the stairs, feet thudding on the carpet, limbs loose and springy. She bounced on the spot in her bedroom and pulled a fresh shirt from her drawer, shaking it out, reluctant to take off Rishona's warm, fragrant leather jacket. She decided on a compromise: the jacket went back on properly over her clean shirt and she swapped her torn leggings for her jeans. Rishona laughed when Tuli sashayed into the kitchen, asking, "Does this look suit me?"

"Better than the muddy leggings and fawn parka outfit you had on earlier. That idiot poacher probably thought you were a deer." Rishona waved her phone. "I ordered pizza since there was none in the freezer. It'll be here in an hour."

Tuli tiptoed across the tiles to find the slippers she had kicked off hours earlier. "We could have had baked potatoes after all."

"Want me to cancel the pizza?" With a laugh, Tuli shook her head and slipped the leather jacket from her shoulders. Rishona pointed at it. "You can keep that on if you're cold. You look cute. Not at all like a dangerous, fire-breathing shapeshifter."

"About that." Tuli gave a little flick of her hair and watched with an *Oh!* on her lips as scales skittered across her hands then vanished as if absorbed into her skin. "What's wrong with me? Why is this happening?" Surprised by the dizzying intensity of her emotions, Tuli blinked rapidly and squeezed her fists tightly closed, hoping to prevent tears. She was too big to cry, she told herself. Crying didn't solve anything.

"Hey, hey you're okay." Rishona stepped over and wrapped Tuli in a hug. "You're not ill or sick or anything, so I don't want you worrying about that. I bet you have a ton of questions. Look, we can eat pizza and watch a film and talk. I'm staying because I don't want you left alone with this."

Tuli leaned into Rishona's embrace, focusing on the cadence and softness of her voice more than the words. She slipped her arms around Rishona's waist and rested her cheek on her shoulder. Rishona's breath eased warmth through her hair and a slight tickle and pressure of a kiss against her neck made Tuli's skin prickle and her pulse pick up. She stayed still, waiting for the older girl to laugh and push her away, ruffle her hair, order her to get homework out, offer a lecture on biology. Waiting for Rishona to tell her what to do next.

But Tuli knew after a full minute that she wasn't going to say anything or move away or laugh, just hold on to her for as long as she needed it, and that was the moment that tipped Tuli from barely holding her tears in check to a state of noisy, rib-heaving sobs.

Rishona held her around the shoulders and crooned gentle words against her hair. After a while, Tuli's sobbing subsided and in the leaden silence that followed, she felt Rishona's chest moving in deep breaths. Tuli straightened up, wiped at her face with a sleeve then realized with embarrassment that she had just used Rishona's leather jacket to dry her face. She muttered an apology and rubbed the leather on her jeans. Rishona laughed softly and Tuli looked at her face at last. Rishona's eyes glistened with tears and streaks tracked down from her eyes too. Tuli found a watery smile. "Look at us," she said, sniffing and reaching for the box of tissues that sat on the windowsill. "Pair of crybabies. Sorry about your jacket."

"It's seen worse," Rishona replied, patting her own puffy eyes with her shirt sleeves. "You wouldn't put it anywhere near your face if you knew how many flies died on it during an average ride."

Tuli looked at the leather in horror, then slipped the jacket off her shoulders and hung it over the back of a chair while Rishona giggled until she got hiccups.

Tuli laughed, then her face opened in delight as an idea pushed all her horror aside for now. "Risho-o-ona-a-a," she sang. "You could show me how to ride your bike sometime. I don't mean go anywhere," she added, seeing the look of horror on Rishona's face. "I just mean up and down the drive."

"You'd fall off." Rishona turned away.

"I bet you fell off at first too."

"That's irrelevant. That was my decision to learn."

"And this is my decision. I could just phone up somewhere and book lessons, you know. I'm old enough. I could buy my own bike and–"

"All right!" Rishona held her hands up in defeat. "Not tonight. You don't have a helmet."

Tuli smiled with as much innocence as she could muster. "But what if I did?"

Rishona raised one eyebrow at Tuli. "Well? Do you?"

Tuli laughed and ran from the kitchen, feet thundering on the stairs. When she returned, she had a plain white crash helmet jammed on her head. Rishona scoffed. "You're not wearing it right. Come here." Tuli trotted over. Rishona adjusted the straps, waggled the helmet and adjusted the straps again. "There," she announced, giving the dome a gentle slap. "Comfortable?"

"Not really." Tuli's voice was slightly muffled because of the helmet's snug fit. Rishona laughed.

"It fits, then. Maybe in the morning I'll show you how to start the bike."

Satisfied for now, Tuli eased off her helmet and set it on the table. Rishona made tea to fill the gap between this moment and the pizza delivery. She sat, placing two steaming mugs down. "So," Tuli said after a moment of gazing into her tea. "If I'm not ill, what's wrong with me?"

"Nothing," Rishona replied immediately. "My gran thinks it's inherited. That's why I wanted to study biology and genetics at college. I want to get a job as a diagnostic genetic technologist in a hospital. You know," Rishona smiled at Tuli's confused expression. "Genome sequencing, find out which combinations of genes are responsible for which conditions, maybe get into gene editing and gene therapy in future."

"So it's genetics?" Tuli frowned across her mug as she took a sip of tea. "So mum or dad has it too?"

"No." Rishona shook her head. "If they did, they'd know what to do to help you adjust. The right combination of genes has probably been lurking here and there dotted around your family tree for generations, all waiting to get together in the same person." Rishona met Tuli's gaze and held it. "In you."

"Gene editing," Tuli leaned forwards, eyes wide. Rishona matched her pose. "So if you know which genes are causing this, you could fix them? Make it stop?"

Tuli sat back with a sigh when Rishona looked away and shook her head. "In theory, maybe. In practice, I don't even know where to start looking for which genes are involved. It's like your eye color. Maybe there's only one or two genes involved. Maybe there are dozens. Maybe there are some environmental factors too that we've not even guessed at yet."

"But you could find them." Tuli spoke as if this was already fact. Rishona sighed again and shook her head. "Do you want to look up how many genes are in the human genome? It would take a lifetime of research, more, probably, to pin down which ones mattered and figure out how to alter them without causing accidental mutations that caused worse problems."

Tuli scraped her chair back, got up and thumped her empty mug into the sink. "Worse than breaking out in scales and talons and roasting alive anyone who gets me angry?" She whirled around to face Rishona, waves of gold and green pulsing up her neck and down her arms. She noticed, clenched her fists, closed her amber-flecked eyes and took a deep breath and held it. "I am not angry," she said through gritted teeth. "I am just so fucking—"

Two things prevented Tuli from bursting outside to vent flames of frustration. First, Rishona's arms were around her again. Second, the roar of another bike and the crunch of boots on gravel heralded the arrival of their pizza.

Outburst suspended, Tuli waited out of sight while Rishona went out to meet the delivery biker. While Rishona exchanged friendly chat with the stranger, Tuli rubbed her arms from shoulder to wrists and stroked her hair, shaking it out. She checked her reflection in the stained-glass panel beside the front door. Normal, she thought. You look perfectly normal. She tightened her lips, sighed, and realized with a guilty start that she was disappointed.

"Come and eat!" Rishona's call summoned Tuli from her introspection. She walked through to the kitchen to find that Rishona was setting up a film in the living room, pizza box sitting on a cloth draped over the footstool. "Want to pick a different one?" Rishona waved the remote at the screen where *Reign of Fire* waited to start. Tuli stared in disbelief then burst out laughing.

"Oh my god, are you fucking kidding me?"

"Language!" Rishona pulled a stern face then laughed too. "I'm kidding. Just think, in a few years you'll be able to watch shows with dragons in them and point out all the bits they get wrong."

"I'd sound like my dad when mum puts science fiction films on." Tuli took a slice of pizza. "A pain in the arse. Go on then," she said, waving at the screen with the pointy end of her pizza. "Let's see poor dragons just trying to survive despite constant attacks from humans. Shit! Wait," Tuli put her pizza down and looked aghast at Rishona. "Am I even human?"

"Yes." Rishona lounged back on the sofa. "Just as human as anyone else with any other random collection of inherited genes. Eat your pizza before it gets cold."

Tuli reclaimed her pizza and reclined beside Rishona. "At least," she murmured as the film started, choosing her moment, "if dinner gets cold I can warm it up from here."

Rishona's cough and splutter made her hoot with laughter.

Tuli ate and watched and asked questions. Rishona answered as best she could. Although she knew that all Rishona was offering was reassurance without any real depth of knowledge or experience to back it up, Tuli felt better from having someone she could talk to. She paused the film halfway to clear away the pizza box and offer to make more tea. "I should call or text mum and let her know," she said, looking thoughtful as odd pieces of conversations with Lydia slotted together into one whole picture. "Mum knows, right?"

Rishona nodded and moved a finger in a circular motion around her own face. "Your mum picked me because I saw you break out in scales when I came for the interview and I didn't scream or panic. And because we'd met before, so I already knew at least a bit about you."

Tuli sighed. "Everyone knew but me. Everyone's seen my other side but me. Mum, dad, Jack and Jamie, you, some random poacher in the forest…they all know what I look like when…when I…" Tuli frowned as she tried to find the right word. "You know what I mean. I don't know what I even look like."

Rishona frowned then shrugged. "I'm not going to make you angry or upset just to get a photo," she said, following Tuli into the kitchen and getting the milk from the fridge. "We could go to my gran's. She might know what to do and her facility has cameras that would record the whole thing if you were curious."

"No." Tuli dropped teabags into two mugs. "Mum didn't send me there when this all started. I want to find out why first."

"Fair enough." Rishona rested her arm across the back of Tuli's shoulders while they waited for the kettle to boil. "She's a good person, though. She really does care about the people she studies."

"People," Tuli said as the kettle clicked off. "Are there more dragons like me there?"

"No. You're very rare, like one in a billion rare. There are probably only a handful like you in the whole world. She's looking after a minotaur, but she's a cow." Rishona pulled Tuli closer with a quick squeeze of the arm around her shoulder, then moved her arm down to Tuli's waist for a moment before letting go. "Gran really wants to meet you."

Tuli finished making tea and slid a mug closer to Rishona. "I'll talk to mum tomorrow and see what she thinks. To be honest, I need to decide what I think first." After a few seconds, Tuli set her mug down so hard the tea sloshed, pointed at Rishona then at the window, a look of joyful realization lighting her face. She opened her laptop. "Cameras! We've got security cameras outside the house. Maybe they recorded something."

Tuli opened the security camera app while Rishona watched over her shoulder, a warm, welcome weight against her back. She leaned back slightly and wrapped Rishona's arm around her waist. Rishona hugged Tuli while the video thumbnails loaded.

"Shit!" Tuli leaned closer to the screen, pointing and frowning. "Look, there's you arriving at five twenty-seven and going out again at five thirty." Tuli jabbed a forefinger at the next video. "This one is you going out when the pizza arrived. There's nothing in between."

"Maybe the cameras just didn't pick up anything," Rishona suggested.

"Or maybe mum deleted those to keep it a secret from me." Tuli slid her phone from her pocket. "I'll ask."

"Wait." Rishona put her hand on Tuli's, over her phone screen. "Are you ready for that conversation with your mum? Right now?"

Tuli sighed at her phone. She opened her texts and typed: *Hi mum, Rishona staying over. We're fine. Love you.* "No," she said after snapping a smiling selfie, sending it and replying blandly to a few more concerned messages from Lydia. "I'm having fun, despite all this…" She waved her hands around and turned to face Rishona. "This *stuff.* Are you okay?"

Rishona smiled and stroked Tuli's hair. "I wouldn't want to miss any of this for anything. Tuli, if I tell you something, will you promise not to hate me for it?"

Tuli frowned at her friend. "What is it? Are you going home tonight after all? I'd be disappointed but I don't think I'd hate you."

"No. I'm not leaving." Rishona took both of Tuli's hands and looked into her eyes, face pensive. "I turned the cameras off earlier. It wasn't your mum deleting the videos. I didn't want her to see and worry about you and…"

Tuli waited a few seconds but Rishona looked away. "And what, Rishona?"

"And take you away from me."

Rishona wrapped her arms around Tuli. "I don't hate you either," Tuli said quietly, holding on a little tighter. "It's probably better that mum didn't see that. She's got enough on her plate as it is."

Tuli led Rishona back into the living room and the girls settled on the sofa to watch the rest of the film. The combination of a stressful day, plenty of food, and a warm companion made Tuli drift into a doze, shaking herself awake when the credits rolled. "Did I miss anything good?" she asked, yawning and stretching.

"The dragons promised to stop eating people if the humans promised to stop attacking them. It was all very amicable, and the two species lived harmoniously side by side forevermore," Rishona said dryly. "Bedtime."

Tuli grinned. "Saturday tomorrow." She picked up the remote to return to the TV menu screen.

"Don't care." Rishona claimed the remote after a short tussle. She turned off the TV.

"Okay," Tuli groaned, "I'm going. Because I want to and I'm tired. Not because I'm told to."

Rishona followed Tuli upstairs, said goodnight with a hug and a kiss on the cheek, and went into Lydia's bedroom. Tuli considered whether to suggest again that Rishona share with her, then shook her head and went into her own room. Despite her conviction that having Rishona in the house would make her lie awake, head whirling with ideas, she was asleep within minutes of starting a fantasy in which Rishona came to her room to complain that her mum's room was too cold and to tell her to budge over.

Morning arrived late. Tuli woke up confused, almost yelled "Mum?" then remembered that the person clattering around on the kitchen was Rishona. She catapulted out of bed, threw on her robe, rammed her feet into slippers and only just remembered to go into the bathroom to brush her teeth before going downstairs. "Good morning," Tuli said, smiling at the sight of Rishona with bed-hair and no makeup. "You look wonderful."

Rishona laughed. "Piss off."

"No, you do." Tuli wrapped her arms around Rishona's waist from behind and leaned for a few seconds. "Thanks for staying over."

"Good morning, then," Rishona said, turning to hug Tuli back, giving and receiving a kiss on the cheek. "How soon can you be ready for your first bike lesson?"

Tuli shrieked, hugged Rishona harder, and raced back upstairs to change into her heaviest jeans, boots and a thick jacket. She came back down to find Rishona looking more alert with combed hair and, although devoid of her usual mascara and lipstick, every bit as composed as usual. "We can't go out beyond the end of the lane unless you have a license."

"I don't have it yet."

"All right. I'll show you how to start the bike and what all the controls are, then I'll take you for a ride." Tuli pushed her helmet onto her head and grinned. Rishona grinned back. "I think your mum'll fire me if she finds out."

"I'm not telling if you're not. I don't tell her everything." She frowned for a second. "And neither do you."

Rishona shook her head. "I tell her you're okay, you're safe and—" She frowned back at Tuli. "Look, about the security cameras. I always cover the motion sensors to deactivate them when I think you're… the other you. I don't want Lydia to worry, and I don't want anyone else to see. Those systems aren't very secure. Lydia's password is your date of birth backwards."

Tuli stiffened, horrified by the thought that someone might be able to eavesdrop on her camera feed. Then she relaxed and smiled sweetly. "I'll try that password on the broadband later."

Rishona led Tuli out and pointed to all the controls on her bike, demonstrated how to check it over, then start it. With a nod, she signaled Tuli to get on and copy her. Tuli cheered when the bike roared into life before idling quietly, then giggled with delight as the engine roared again when she twisted the throttle. "Can I ride it to the end of the drive?"

"You can try," Rishona laughed. "Okay, where did I say the clutch was?"

A frisson run up and down Tuli's back as the bike moved off. She looked at her hands to locate the clutch again so she could change up a gear and grabbed for the front brake in alarm. The bike sputtered and died. "You're okay," Rishona said. "Close your eyes. Take a deep breath. Focus on what you want."

"This is going to get in the way of riding," Tuli said as her talons retracted and her hands returned to the shape she called normal.

"But you're learning to control it." Rishona put one hand on the handlebars and tapped Tuli's shoulder. "You can get on behind me. Hold on to me and you won't fall off. I won't let you."

Tuli nodded. Rishona showed Tuli how to sit, then sat forward and Tuli slid into place behind her. With a quick yell of "Two taps if you need me to stop!" Rishona set off along the little road at a sedate pace that felt, to Tuli, as exhilarating as if they were soaring.

It wasn't supposed to be a long ride. At the end of the road the farm lane joined the main road. Rishona followed the main road east for a couple of miles then pulled off onto one of the forestry tracks, rode slowly through the trees and rejoined the main road further on, this time turning west to go back home. Tuli clung on, concentrating on the feeling of freedom and the feeling of Rishona's hips against the insides of her thighs and the feeling of scales skittering up and down her back. At the bend in the lane where Tuli's cottage could be glimpsed between the trees, Rishona stopped, killed the engine, and pointed. Tuli's breath caught in horror at the sight of a Land Rover and a van in the drive and three figures in camouflage gear and balaclavas, all holding shotguns, walking into her home. Rishona shushed her. As silently as possible, Rishona motioned for Tuli to get off, got off too, and pushed the bike back along the lane and up a deer-trodden path into the forest.

Once safely hidden by the trees, Rishona and Tuli took their helmets off and sat beside the bike, hidden by tall, winter-browned bracken, looking pensively at each other.

"I'm calling the police." Tuli pulled her phone out of her inside jacket pocket and cursed at it. "No signal. Typical."

"They'd probably tell you to stay out of the way until someone can get here in an hour or two. Look, I know you're not keen, but we should go to my gran's. You can call the police from there."

Tuli got to her feet. "We could go up to the village and see if the signal is better. Mum'll be furious if they take all our stuff."

Rishona stared at her for a few seconds then got up too. "I don't think they're after your TV and spare cash. Tuli, I think they're after you."

Tuli felt her scales shiver up her back and shoulders. "I could," she said, then stopped, surprised by the deeper, rougher sound of her voice. She swallowed and closed her eyes, concentrating on the calmness of the forest around her. "I could deal with them," she said more quietly, opening her eyes and checking her hands. "I could get closer and–"

"And get shot or captured. No, Tuli, you can't risk it."

"I'd be okay. You've seen what I can do."

Rishona shook her head hard enough to make her hair dance around her shoulders. "Please, don't." She threw her arms around Tuli, who stiffened in surprise. "If you got hurt...we just...I don't want to lose you, okay?"

Tuli slipped her arms around Rishona's waist. She rested her cheek on Rishona's shoulder for a few seconds, then raised it again when she felt Rishona stir. Their eyes met and Tuli found that she couldn't look away. The shushing of the breeze-blown boughs above their heads seemed to die away to nothing as Tuli brought one hand up to stroke Rishona's loose hair back from her face. Rishona's voice was barely a whisper above the wind. "I couldn't bear to lose you."

Tuli murmured back, "You won't lose me," then kissed Rishona on the cheek. She waited for the barest instant in case Rishona pushed away, ready to get moving, but she held on. Tuli smiled, then pressed her lips to Rishona's.

Rishona held Tuli even more tightly and chased her for another kiss when she broke the brief contact between them. This time, Tuli looped her arm around Rishona's neck and held on, catching Rishona's lower lip between her own and feeling a hot tingle deep in her gut as she pushed her body as close as she could get. She felt Rishona's tongue against her upper lip, pulled back and giggled. "I wish we'd done this before. Like, last night on the sofa."

Rishona laughed. "Believe me, I was thinking about it. It didn't seem like the right moment."

"I'm not sure this is the right moment either, but I don't care." Tuli leaned in for another kiss, this time with a little more confidence, and Rishona met her halfway.

"We need," Rishona murmured between soft kisses, "To go. To gran's."

Tuli released her with reluctance. "I want to check out home first. Quietly, I promise. See if they're gone. Do you think they'll have gone?"

Rishona shrugged. "I didn't hear any cars go past on the road. Did you?"

Tuli laughed and shook her head. "I wasn't exactly listening." She looked around the familiar arrangement of mature trunks, picking out a route that would bring them to a slight rise opposite the cottage. "There's a spot where we'll be able to see the cottage without anyone seeing us. This way."

Rishona followed, hauling the bike as far as one of the rough forestry roads that crisscrossed the ranks of trees, leaving it there ready for their escape. After that the girls crept as quietly as possible to Tuli's vantage point, staying below the crest of the low hill, moving back and forth to find the best place to peer out from the relative safety of the gloom between the trunks. The van was gone, but the Land Rover remained, with one man in army surplus camouflage gear waiting at the gate. A shout came from their right and, to Tuli's dismay, an answer from their left. "We need to go!" Rishona's whisper hissed in the wind. "Now!"

Tuli was already on her feet, but crouching. She kicked off her boots and shed her jacket but there was nothing she could do about the stretching and tearing of her shirt and her jeans. Fury drove her, but also, like a calming layer on top of her desperation, the desire to live her life unbothered and the hope that Rishona would stay with her. She launched herself vertically with a leap from powerful leg muscles, scrabbled for grip until her talons caught on wrinkled bark, then leapt again from her perch until she was at the treetops and could unfold her wings. She circled once, seeing Rishona run and stumble and run again. Her sharp eyes picked out the movement of a camouflage-clad hunter tramping through her forest to the east and another to the west. She shrieked down at one, watching with glee as he splashed into a ditch between the young trees in a newer part of the plantation, then turned on the other and chased him deeper into the heart of the forest where ancient oaks and beeches and hornbeams marked the end of the plantation and the start of the last vestiges of old forest that had been part the land since before humans arrived.

She headed home and landed on the patchy lawn, wings folding back and hips adjusting to her human gait. The Land Rover was gone and all that Tuli could detect of the man left to stand guard was a stench of tobacco smoke and stale beer. Rishona's bike came around the corner too fast and wobbled, but Rishona corrected and roared up to the cottage, braking sharply and skidding on the gravel. On the concrete patio Tuli pulled off the shreds that remained of her torn clothing. She extended her elongated arms and watched as the leathery flaps that joined her hands to her shoulders and back resolved once more into wings. She gave a few experimental flaps, not enough to lift her from but enough to give her the sense that if she chose, she could launch herself into the air and not come down.

Rishona staggered back as Tuli almost knocked her over with a careless wingbeat. "No, Tuli, you can't. They must have seen you. Shit, Tuli, don't do this. Let's go inside and get you some clothes then get out of here again. You can't risk getting caught!"

Tuli stretched her wings out and up as far as they would go, feeling the pins-and-needles itch and tingle ease as blood vessels filled and pressure on new nerves lessened. She tried a few more shallow, lazy flaps and let out a whoop of delight that lit up the sky. On the next flap, stronger and faster, her feet lost contact with the ground. It would be so easy, she thought, to do this deliberately. Without anger or fear or hurt to force her instincts. With a little more effort, she could soar above the treetops and if anyone tried to hurt her she could rain fire down on them. She could fly all the way to London and–

And why not further? Who could possibly stop her? With one more roar of delight, Tuli launched herself upwards. She spiraled up and up, grazing the clouds and shivering at their damp chill. She looked down, seeing the world beneath her laid out like a map. There was the cottage, a gray L-shape set in a rectangle of pale green grass and beige gravel. There was her forest, dark green fronds swishing over brown-black shadows. There was the single-track road, a dark gray ribbon curving around the forest and past the cottage. And there was a red dot traveling along it, Rishona, following on her bike, a flash of pale face glancing up when she dared, bike veering dangerously close to a drainage ditch on the side of the road and then tumbling in. Something bloomed in Tuli's chest, something warm and wanting, and she circled lazily down until her feet were running across rough grass cropped short by hungry livestock.

She reached Rishona as she was pulling her bike upright and cursing. "This is your fault, you know, taking off like that. I could barely keep you in sight." Rishona brushed at the grazes on her leathers. "Good job there wasn't anything else on the road. My bike's ruined. Something's jammed and I can't even push it. I'll have to call someone to pick us up."

"That was not my fault," Tuli replied, smiling at Rishona. "You didn't have to follow. I'd've come back for you." Her face dropped into concern. "Seriously, though, are you okay? Did you hurt yourself?"

Rishona shook herself out and rubbed at her arms and legs. "I wasn't going all that fast. I'm a bit shaken up, but I'm not hurt. I'll have some bruises, but my leathers did their job. I'll call someone and–"

Tuli leapt and enfolded Rishona in a warm hug, leathery wings making a cocoon around her, elongated, clawed fingers scratching gently at Rishona's hair then settling to a comforting scrape of fingernails as Tuli's form altered back to something human enough to pass at a glance. "I'm not going to your gran's. I won't be kept safe like that, hidden away. I'll keep myself safe."

Rishona let her forehead drop against Tuli's. She closed her eyes and took a deep breath. "I'm scared you'll disappear and I'll never know what happened to you. Maybe you'll fly too high or too far and get lost or someone will…or something. Something else." Rishona glared into Tuli's amber-flecked gaze. "Don't do that to me."

Tuli felt Rishona's anger in the stiffening of her embrace, heard it in the sharp intake of breath, and sensed it in the warmth of her cheeks. "I won't," Tuli said. "I won't leave you behind again." She straightened and stretched out her arms, watching Rishona's look of wonder as she willed her wings to spread and her talons to grow and her scales to cover her with green-gold armor.

"Get on," Tuli growled, less surprised as she became more familiar with the timbre of her voice. "I can carry us both." Rishona looked doubtful. "You want to walk? Put your arms around my neck and when I'm off the ground, put your legs around my hips. Squeeze twice if you need to stop. I won't let you fall off. I promise."

Rishona glanced at her wrecked bike, looked both ways up and down the road, now black in the fast fading twilight, let her eyes rove over half-changed Tuli for a moment, then sighed and put her helmet back on. "You probably owe me a new helmet too," she grumbled, but by the time she gripped tightly around Tuli's neck, a smile had lifted her face.

Tuli stretched her wings as far as she could and tested her range of movement with Rishona behind her. It wasn't perfect, but once she was up, and Rishona lost her fear and relaxed, it would be easier. She lumbered through the gate into the field, powerful thigh muscles bearing Rishona's weight as easily as her own, hip and knee joints changing their angle to fit her dragon form, clawed feet finding firm purchase in the permanent pasture. Tuli ran. And as she ran, her wings caught the wind until she felt like the heaviest weight in the world could not have kept her feet on the ground. She leapt. Then she was soaring once more, flapping her wings hard at first as she climbed, feeling the wet, cold mist of the low fog on her face, rising higher and higher until she breached the cloud tops and saw a shining crescent moon and pinprick stars scattered like glitter above. Behind her, Rishona laughed and screamed and whooped. Rishona yelled in Tuli's ear, "Where are we going?"

Confident that nobody on the ground would see them above the clouds and that nobody flying high would bother to look down, Tuli let out a long jet of blue-orange flame. She laughed too and shook her head. "Anywhere," she roared back over the whistling wind. "Anywhere we want."

THE
MYSTERY OF
AXTON MANSION

When his phone blares out the opening theme from The X-Files, Alexander Yorke, Paranormal Investigator, Freelance Writer, and The Black Country's best-known Skeptical Podcaster, closes his pale blue eyes, crosses his slender fingers and hopes. Using a little sense and a little science to explain reports of hauntings and expose charlatans who prey on the still-raw grief of those who have lost loved ones, makes Alex's work moderately popular with stalwarts of the skeptical community, but not popular enough to bring in much revenue from the few regular advertising slots in his podcast. He needs a job that pays cash.

He grins and lets out a little hissed *yesss!* when the screen lights up with a photo of a smiling woman with warm, brown skin, close-cropped, tight, black curls, and the name Paulina Hughes. She's been a friend since Alex wrote for the university magazine she edited, now she runs the local newspaper. Silently he hopes for a commission, but right now he'd settle for a free lunch.

He answers the call to hear her traditional bellow of, "Hey babe! Got something for you if you're not busy."

"Hi Paulina, you want an article?" he asks, raking his hand through his hair to push the floppy blond strands off his pale, freckled face. "I can write you something fast or I can write you something with depth."

"Depth, please. I have plenty of other people who can do fast. I want you to investigate a haunting. It's local, a house. Belongs to a mate of mine. She bought it cheap and fixed it up, but it's been empty for ages because people get 'a creepy, unwelcoming feeling' from the bedroom. I need a piece for the weekend supplement. Twenty-five inches at union rates with a bonus if you actually find a ghost and have it ready for the Halloween edition."

Alex tightens his lips, grips his free hand into a fist, does mental arithmetic and thinks it over. He wouldn't be able to use the article for his podcast until Paulina said he could, but he'd get paid for about a thousand words, enough to cover a decent chunk of rent for his one-bed flat.

"C'mon Alex," Paulina cajoles. "You do great research for your articles and you love hauntings. Do this one thing. Find a ghost for me. It's a nice house, babe. A bit eighties, but in good nick. Two bedrooms, fitted wardrobes, radiators." She pauses then lowers her voice. "What if your deposit and first month's rent count as…" Her tone turns sing-song. "…research expenses?"

"You want me to live there?" Alex closes his eyes and sighs into the phone. "For how long? I can't afford two rents, Paulie. I can only just afford this place on my own since Jas–"

"Oh!" Paulina cuts him off. "Leave that boxy little dump and just move there. The rent's very reasonable for the area and you get so much more for your money when you're out of the center." Paulina waits for a silent count of three then says, voice tentatively cheerful, "You've not said no. Does that mean it's a yes?" There's another brief pause then Paulina whoops. "It's a yes!"

"Fine, yes, okay," Alex tries to keep the enthusiasm out of his reply now that the idea of moving out, leaving good and bad memories behind, has gripped him more securely. "I'll do it. Please don't be disappointed when all I find is creaky stairs and dodgy central heating."

"It's a bungalow and the boiler is still under guarantee. Come and discuss the details over lunch. One o'clock? At the 'Bell, Book and Candle?'"

Alex laughs. "For the two-for-one beer and curry deal? Cheapskate."

"Cheeky! The Gazette generously agreed to pay your rent for a month." Paulina laughs back. "Are you too fancy for us plebs in print now you have your own paranormal podcast?"

Alex laughs again and shakes out his hand to make his fist relax. "One o'clock. See you. Bye, Paulie."

Alex is still grinning when Paulina texts him the address. He taps at his laptop and looks up the house he's agreed to investigate. In all of his podcasts so far, his clients have turned out to be haunted by no more than insect infestations, rat-chewed wiring, settling timbers and cranky plumbing. They have almost always been disappointed to find out there is a repair bill rather than a ghost.

But this house looks different. For a start, it's not the usual creepy, crumbling Victorian pile or Georgian townhouse or Edwardian terrace. Chills that trail icy fingertips across the nape of the neck are explained away by draughts from poorly fitting windows. Whispers behind walls are explained by the hissing of water past mineral buildup inside ancient lead pipes. Phantom footsteps are attributed to the cracking and creaking of wooden floorboards, shrinking and settling as the house temperature slowly drops after sundown. This house is not even particularly old. It's a squat, post-war bungalow on the grounds of an estate that the local nobility couldn't afford to keep as attitudes modernized, unlike the renovated mansion. It's a perfectly ordinary, neat little two-bed-one-bath home.

Except nobody wants to stay there. According to Paulina's follow-up email, it's getting a reputation for being uninhabitable even at well below the usual rent for the genteel estate where it nestles in its little garden, between two more identical houses in a group set comfortably back from the road. Alex scans his gaze over the property description with an interest rooted less in professional concerns, and more in the growing domestic desire to live in a nice house. But if Paulina wants him to investigate a local haunting and will pay well for a ghost story for her newspaper, and the owners will pay him for proving that there is no ghost, it doesn't matter whether his research pleases Paulina more or the owners. He wins either way.

When he calls the agency for more information, a cheerful voice offers to show him around the property that afternoon. It's only a few stops out of town on the bus and Alex arrives just as the agent is getting out of her car. They exchange polite smiles and handshakes.

"Alex Yorke."

"I know. The ghost hunter. I'm Claire. I listen to your show sometimes."

Alex smiles his thanks but holds back from asking her what she thinks of his podcast. She looks at the house, looks meaningfully at Alex, then hands him the keys.

"You go ahead. I'll wait in the car."

"I see," Alex says drily. "Wouldn't want to annoy the dead but not yet departed. Do you mind if I record some notes while I'm in there?"

Claire's eyes open wide and her lips part. "You're investigating? You believe there really is a ghost?" She leans closer and whispers. "There is! I know it. You could interview me for your podcast."

Alex shakes his head. "There are no such things as ghosts. I promise. I'll find problems with the electrics or the plumbing or the gas, or maybe something in the attic." Claire gasps softly and her pink cheeks turn pale. "I mean birds or mice," Alex clarifies.

"All the same." The young agent's face falls. "I'll wait out here."

Alex huffs in exasperation, takes the keys and walks up the crazy-paving path that bisects a lawn studded with dandelions. He readies his voice-to-text app and goes inside.

The house has the same sad, uninviting air as every other long-vacant property he has investigated. It's not quite warm enough without actually being cold, every sound echoes from the bare walls as if the house is talking to itself, and the hallway smells of a mixture of fresh paint and old dog. There is a plug-in air freshener doing its best to cover it all with lavender.

He starts by examining all the windows and doors, then he checks that all the taps work and listens at the walls for the telltale *shushashushashush* of water pushing past a blockage. Next, he checks the gas appliances for leaks and for flames burning smoky yellow instead of pale blue, a sign of incomplete combustion that might lead someone to become light-headed and delirious from low level carbon monoxide poisoning. After that, he turns off every appliance and waits for his ears to adjust to the mains hum pervading every human space, then he turns lights and sockets on and off one at a time listening carefully for extra pops, buzzes and crackles. Last of all, he walks around outside checking the ventilation blocks in the walls are not covered over and looking for any sign of infestation by rats or insects. There has to be something wrong with the house, he dictates confidently into his phone. Something fixably mundane.

But that's just it. He can't find anything obviously wrong with the house at all. It's far nicer than his noisy little place in town but, as Paulina promised, not much more expensive, and if she is paying for a month that almost evens it out. Alex does the calculations again in his head and flashes a grin at the twin windows that watch him from the back of the house. He could do much worse than to move here. He goes back inside for one more look around. The kitchen is at the front, small and cheerful with a rectangular window, yellow walls and pine cabinets that have seen better days. The living room is opposite, across the entrance hallway, inoffensively bland in shades of beige he could dress up with bright throws and curtains. The smaller bedroom at the back would make a great study, and there's no through-the-wall neighbor to interrupt him with unwanted noise when he's recording. The bathroom, squeezed between the kitchen and the smaller bedroom, has a faded peach-colored suite with an electric shower over a smallish bath. The main bedroom makes him shiver with damp and cold, but when he looks closely at the corners and slides the polished wooden doors of the wardrobe open, there is no telltale yellow staining or peeling wallpaper or black spotty mold so he expects a few days of decent ventilation and heating will lift the chill.

A narrow passageway squeezes between the bedrooms and ends in a glazed door that leads out into a privet-bordered garden, overgrown from a summer or two of neglect. As he looks out from the main bedroom window, misting with condensation from his breath, Alex imagines spring flowers, summer barbecues and warm autumn evenings with beers on the lawn. He shivers and rubs his arms, huffs out a laugh, excited at the prospect of moving into a proper, grown-up house. He leans closer to the window and breathes on the glass to extend the little patch of mist he's made and draws a heart on the pane before he turns to leave. The temperature seems to lift a little as he steps away from the window. "I'll take it," he murmurs as he imagines talking to the agent. "There's no ghost but you can't increase the rent until the lease runs out."

A sudden draught makes the hairs on the back of his neck stand up but Alex rubs it away without a second thought. As he leaves the house, locking the front door behind him, he sees Claire leaning against her car, tapping at her phone. "Claire? Hi. Yes. I'll take it."

Startled, Claire jumps out of her slouch. "You'll—oh! Are you sure? Okay. I, um, left the paperwork at the office." She treats Alex to a hair flick and a little laugh. "I didn't think you'd actually take this place on."

"Give me a lift back, then. I want a twelve-month lease. Deposit and first months' rent to be paid by the Gazette. But I won't pay more than—" Alex names a monthly figure just a little less than the asking price, "—on account of the state of the garden."

Claire pulls a face then shrugs and nods. "I should argue with that, but I can't see there being a problem since it's been empty for so long. I bet the owners will just be glad someone wants to live here." She laughs again, a slightly nervous sound. "And I never want to have to show this creepy old dump again. Your boss at the Gazette already called to authorize payment if you agreed to take the place and they emailed a reference so all I need is your bank details and some ID."

She unlocks the car and Alex gets in the passenger seat. Claire fastens her seatbelt, starts the engine and looks at Alex seriously. "Last time I showed this place to someone, the ghost took my pen."

"The ghost took your pen," Alex echoes, allowing a trace of derision to seep into his voice.

Claire frowns defensively. "It did! I swear. I left it on the kitchen worktop with the paperwork. When we got back to the kitchen after looking at all the rooms the pen was gone, and the ghost had scrawled 'NO' on the contract. Never found it again."

"Well then," Alex smiles brightly. "When I find the ghost, I'll ask it to give your pen back."

Alex signs the lease and collects the keys at closing time the same day. He returns to his new home as soon as he can for another look around, taking his torch and a small stepladder with him. He talks to his phone while he examines every window for gaps in the fittings that would allow draughts to whistle and moan, but the double glazing is well-fitted and still under warranty. The boiler makes occasional eerie howling noises, but Alex calls a heating engineer who promises it's a simple blockage and they'll be round to fix it tomorrow. There are no creaking floorboards. Alex peels back the carpet and finds the floors are concrete. There's not even a damp, creepy basement, and when he walks around the outside and looks up at the roof line he sees the chimney has been capped, so there shouldn't be any crows cawing in the rafters.

Forcing the painted-shut loft hatch, Alex hauls himself up into the chilly attic. He carefully steps over the insulation, moving from joist to joist, to reach the skylight. The glass is cracked and taped over, but it seems secure enough and his flashlight reveals no signs of any skittering, buzzing or flapping residents to make suspicious noises at night.

So there is no reason, no reason at all, for the chill Alex feels again on his neck as he walks into the larger of the two bedrooms, or for the frisson that makes his arm hair stand up as if affected by static electricity.

"Well then," he says, hearing the slightest echo shadow his words in the empty room. He laughs, partly in embarrassment at himself for reacting physically to a ghost story that hasn't been told yet, partly to dispel the creepy feeling tickling up and down his spine. He puts on his clearest, most confident voice, the one Paulina calls his 'podcast accent.' "One knock for yes, two for no, and three for I'd rather not answer." He rattles the wardrobe's sliding door and switches to a spooky, sing-song wail. "Is this house hau-au-au-aunte-e-e-ed?" Scoffing at himself, Alex turns to leave. As soon as his back is to the room, he hears three soft, muffled knocks.

He freezes. He must have imagined it. Misinterpreted the sound of...of...of something else. Maybe something in the kitchen or the bathroom fell over and rolled or bounced. He turns around to face the room, holding his phone tightly in front of him. "Pardon?"

Nothing. Alex forces a laugh and shakes his head. "You're going soft. You don't believe in ghosts." He turns away again. Just as his hand reaches the door knob, very faintly, he hears it.

Thud. Thud. Thud.

He's out of that room in a flash. He searches the entire house, inside and out, for anything that might explain the knocking, treating the empty rooms to a running commentary of everything he's doing just to hear the calm, reassuring sound of his own voice. There is nothing loose in the kitchen. There is no unsecured cable slapping against the outside wall. There isn't even a TV aerial juddering on loose bolts. Nothing.

But he has a point to prove. Although it seems creepy, he knows for sure there will be an explanation for this in the real world and he'll find it. There are no such things as ghosts. And he prides himself that he has a reputation at least as well-known as the house. He returns to the hallway, every door open so he can see into every room. "All right, house," he announced, "I'll be moving in tomorrow and I will find every rattling panel, loose wire, and knocking pipe, and I. Will. Get. Them. *Fixed*."

As soon as he gets back to his flat, which now feels so cramped he wonders how he ever shared it, Alex calls everyone he can think of who might help. Tomas has to work and, since he's a researcher for Paulina, Alex doesn't dare push him to take a sick day. Two other friends promise to help, but only if he can hold off until the weekend. There is one more name in his contacts he can try, but he can't bring himself to phone. Instead, he texts.

Hi Jas can you help me move house? Sorry to ask but I really need your help.

His phone whistles the X-Files theme again. Alex almost drops it in his haste to answer. "You mean," says a sharp voice, "you really need a driver and one of my mum's vans for free."

"Yes please," Alex says quickly, before he backs out, mutters an apology and hangs up. "If you can and if she doesn't mind."

"As it happens, I do have tomorrow afternoon free." Jaspreet's voice softens a little. "But I don't owe you any favors, Alex. You've been ignoring me."

"I know. Sorry. Charge me for your time if you want. Keep it professional. Send an invoice to Paulie at the Gazette. I'm investigating a haunted house for her and I have to live there. For research."

"Huh." Alex waits for a decision in the awkward silence and imagines that familiar face pursing his lips and narrowing his dark brown eyes. Eventually, Jaspreet replies, "Okay. I suppose I can help out. It'll cost you dinner."

"Dinner! Yes." Alex pauses, wary. "It's been ages since we had dinner."

"It has," Jaspreet replies quietly. Alex detects another few degrees of thaw in his tone.

"Yes. Well." Alex bites his lips and breathes through his nose. Once. Twice. Three times, to avoid saying: *six months, Jas, six months and I missed you sometimes, but I had to keep you away to get over this.* Because it won't help. "Thanks. I really appreciate it."

Jaspreet turns up at two in the afternoon, just as Alex is putting the last of his belongings into a cardboard box scrounged from the greengrocer downstairs. It hasn't taken him long to pack up and dismantle the few items of furniture he owns. Between them, Alex and Jaspreet wrestle everything down two flights of stairs and into the back of a van emblazoned with *Kaur's Kitchen Designs*, parked over the curb with its wheels straddling the double yellows, then thank the shopkeeper for being ready to holler at the first glimpse of a traffic warden.

Unloading is even more swift. As they set the sofa down in the living room, the last item, Jaspreet groans and stretches. "At least this place has no stairs. Where are you taking me for dinner?"

"The usual," Alex replies without thinking. "I mean The Seven Locks."

Jaspreet scoffs but smiles. "That'll feel odd." He gives a little shake of his head. "It hasn't been our usual for months and it's not a date."

"Let's get take-out then," Alex suggests. Jaspreet laughs, slouches on the sofa, and a little of the awkwardness lifts.

"Okay. You order. I'll help you put your bed back together. You kept the hex key, right?"

"Taped it to one of the legs." Alex pulls out his phone. "Thai?"

Jaspreet nods and levers himself up from the sofa. Once Alex has ordered food, he joins Jaspreet in the main bedroom and sighs at all the posts and slats and bolts laid out on the carpet. He shivers.

"The other bedroom is warmer. You sure you want to sleep in here?"

Alex watches his breath mist the air. "I swear it just got colder. Okay. I'll use the smaller bedroom until I figure out what's up with the heating in here. Probably an airlock in the pipes or something."

Together they move all the pieces into the smaller bedroom.

Jaspreet picks up the headboard section of the frame and feels down its legs, then repeats with the foot section. "I can't find the hex key. Are you sure you taped it securely?"

"Of course! It's–" Alex frowns. There's tape on one leg, but no tool. "Damn it, it must've fallen out somewhere. I'll get another one tomorrow. The mattress on the floor will have to do for tonight."

Once they have moved the pieces to the side and dropped the mattress, there's nothing else to do but wait for food and eat it at the little drop-leaf table they once knocked knees at in the cramped, town center flat. Every conversation dies out after a couple of sentences, but when the take-out cartons are empty, Jaspreet smiles warmly at Alex. He stands up. "I have to go. Work tomorrow."

"Yeah." Alex returns the smile and stands up too to make eye contact more comfortably. "Thanks for helping me out."

Jaspreet holds Alex's gaze for a couple of seconds. "I'm glad you've decided to move on. You know, when I said I wanted us still to be friends, Al, I meant it."

Don't. Just don't. "Okay." Alex sighs and pushes his hair back from his face. "Good night, Jas."

Jaspreet moves in for a hug, Alex goes for a handshake, and they both laugh it off with neither.

Alone again, Alex walks around his new home one more time before bed. He finds the missing hex key on the main bedroom windowsill and pockets it, but decides the mattress on the floor will still be good enough for one night. He finds the black bag with his bedding in it and makes up his bed the best he can. A hot shower eases the ache from the day's exertion that's beginning to pull at his shoulders. Wearing clean pajamas, he slips into bed, back resting on a pillow propped up against the wall and picks up the novel he has left out for himself. The page doesn't hold his attention so he reads it again, but his eyes are only skimming the words. His phone, always within reach, offers him games. He drops the device three times as fatigue overcomes him, yet he snaps awake with worries that will probably turn out to be trivial gnawing at his mind. He's jittery, he realizes. He's got a noisy head looking for things to fret about and unable to switch off. Sighing, Alex gets up again and pads into the kitchen. "One to take the edge off." He removes a blister pack from its carton, pops out a little white pill and swallows it with a mouthful of water. "Two if I'm still wide awake in half an hour."

He's not. Sleep pulls him comfortably down when he's halfway through a difficult sudoku, and his phone slides safely from his hand to the carpet.

Soft yellow sunlight filters through breeze-shaken leaves, far greener than they should be for the time of year, feeling more like a vivid memory of early summer than the real thing. Birds he can't identify chirp and whistle and hoot from the safety of the trees, and there's water somewhere nearby – he can hear the gentle gurgle of a brook or maybe a fountain – but he can't turn around to see it. Is he lying on grass? He can't tell, but he's calm and comfortable despite the sharp, chill breeze blowing over his skin and prickling his hands and face.

"Who are you?" The voice seems to come from behind him. "This is my place. Why are you here?"

The voice sounds more curious than unwelcoming. "I live here," Alex wants to say but the words won't leave his lips. "This is my place too," he thinks, willing the meaning of his words into existence. "I won't be in your way."

"There was someone else with you."

"Jas." Alex thinks about the man and smiles in his sleep as his memory conjures up warm brown skin, a generous smile and thick, jet black hair. "We thought we were in love, but it didn't work out."

"Oh!"

The surprise in the other voice jerks Alex briefly out of his dream. When he falls asleep again seconds later, his mind is blank, and when his alarm blares, he groans and clicks it off, glad to have had a calm, dreamless night.

Paulina insists on a housewarming party at the weekend and invites a few friends on Alex's behalf. On the very brief tour of his new home, Alex explains that the main bedroom is empty because the second bedroom is cozier. He tells himself that it's not a lie, because although the thermometer he has taped to the wall proves it is not more than a couple of degrees cooler than the rest of the house, every time he goes into the larger bedroom, he feels a chill that shivers his spine, as if directly sapping warmth from his body. After Jaspreet wanders in there and comes out hugging his arms around himself, Alex closes the door.

"Found me a ghost yet?" Paulina's head pops out from the kitchen doorway. She nods at the closed door. "Maybe you talked to the one Jas says lives in there?"

Alex grins at his friend. "I promise I will let you know as soon as I find anything remotely inexplicable by modern science and housing regulations."

"Well, it's a good thing you don't need two bedrooms," Paulina quips, head disappearing back into the living room. "Although you could sublet that room if you weren't so fussy."

"Hey," Jaspreet comes to his defense, "my mum liked that he's house-proud."

"Fussy?" Alex walks in to the living room just as Paulina clicks her glass down on the polished wooden coffee table. He tuts and moves it onto a coaster, wiping the damp ring with his sleeve. "Who's fussy?" he winks at Jas, making him laugh.

The evening passes with music and banter, and everyone takes a joyful turn at making fun of the skeptic's haunted house, but nobody gets drunk enough to have to stay the night. Jaspreet offers to help clear up, but Alex helps him into his coat and chivvies him out to a waiting taxi then collects up the glasses. He washes them in soapy water so hot it makes his hands tingle then rinses in cold and dries them right away with a clean cloth, so they don't smear. He washes and stacks the plates, then wipes down the table surfaces and vacuums up spilled crumbs.

"Fussy!" he scoffs as he surveys his clean living room and

kitchen from the hallway. "There's nothing fussy about wanting to keep things nice."

Fussy.

Alex shakes his head and looks around. A gust of air outside, probably. A crumpled packet rustling as it moves in the kitchen bin. The big bedroom door is open again. He closes it gently.

For a week, nothing unusual happens. Alex researches the area and the history of the Axton family, the previous owners of the mansion that stands at the heart of the estate. It is now a luxurious private care home surrounded by just enough greenery to shield it from prying eyes. Some of his new neighbors work there and they are curious about who might be able to stand up to the resident unsettled spirit. His next-door neighbor, a gray-faced, dour man called Peterson, offers to fill Alex in with all the local gossip about the mansion and its history. Alex agrees with genuine enthusiasm – local color can be a great selling point for an article or maybe even a book about the house – and invites Peterson to come in for coffee. The man laughs and shakes his head. "No way. But you can come to mine."

Peterson's house has a modern feel inside and is far more tastefully decorated than Alex expected from a widower teetering between middle aged and elderly. Over mugs of instant coffee and squares of Battenberg cake, Peterson talks about his job as a caretaker at the mansion, and about the mansion's oldest resident. "The Axtons came with the house, so the story goes. Our Mr Axton was already past his youth when he was forced to sell the land when his father passed away and that was 70 years ago. He's ancient. Mind as sharp as a knife, though, so his nurses say."

Alex shudders. There's a faint chill around the hairline at the back of his neck and he desperately wishes he could ask Peterson to talk about something else. "Who else lived there? At the mansion. Before, I mean?"

Peterson shrugs. "There were servants too, right up until the war took them. My ma said her ma sometimes cleaned for them up at the house. Old Mr Axton was confined to his room by ill health. Nobody was allowed to disturb the old man except his son, who wasn't young either. A family used to come for the summer and rent a cottage, so my grandma cleaned and cooked for them too. They stopped though, after their boy died. My grandma wouldn't let my ma take shortcuts across the grounds after that."

Peterson smiled into his tea cup. "This was her house, you know? My ma's. She was one of the first to move in. Always said grandma would've been proud that she grew up to own a piece of Axton land."

A slight frisson skittering down his spine, tells Alex he has heard something important. "What do you know about them?" he asks as nonchalantly as he can. "The family who came for the summers?"

"Nothing really. Just a name. Unusual. Oz-something. Ozanich."

Alex itches to write it down before he forgets. He resists asking Peterson to agree to an interview for his podcast for the moment, thanks him for the coffee and cake, leaves his number in case the old man remembers or finds out anything more, and goes back to his own house. He writes "Ozanich" on the pad beside his laptop on the kitchen table, then searches the name on the internet and wades through page after page of tediously irrelevant social media profiles.

Frustrated, he calls Paulina. Paulina has never heard the name either, but she immediately suggests that Alex should search the newspaper archives and offers the time of one of her staff.

"Peterson didn't know the dates," Alex says to Tomas, Paulina's least busy researcher, a pale skinned, dark-haired man whose youthful looks disguise his three decades, over the two for one burger and a drink deal at the 'Bell, Book and Candle.' "We should start with 1946 and work forward to 1950 when the estate was sold."

There's only one microfiche reader in the basement archive room. Alex and Tomas take turns at the screen, swapping over when they start to feel seasick, then Tomas checks the films are replaced correctly in their index boxes and returns them safely to the storage room. With the inevitable, fascinating distraction of getting sidetracked to wonder about, or scoff at, local news writers' take on events that now seem like distant history, it takes two people three days to find anything and costs Alex so much in drinks, pub lunches, takeaways and fancy coffee that he considers submitting an expenses claim.

But eventually Alex stares at the tiny notice in the "Hatches, Matches and Dispatches" section of the 4th November 1949 edition. He magnifies it and takes a photo of the blurry screen with his phone.

It's the notice of the death of Harry Ozanich-Strong. Now he has a name, a date and a location. It's a foothold. He goes home after a celebratory drink with Tomas and Paulina. The internet tells him nothing more about the Ozanich-Strong boy, so he decides to visit the local registry office next. He pulls up the photo of the newspaper and reads it aloud to himself as he clunks around the kitchen.

It is with deep sadness that we report the death of Henry (Harry) Ozanich-Strong (21) Loving son and nephew. Funeral 5/11/49 Holy Name Church.

"I should check out if the church still exists," Alex muses as he makes tea. "At least the internet should know that."

He sets his mug on a coaster and pulls his paper pad towards him.

He stares.

Frowns.

Someone has scored out "Ozanich" and written GRIFFIN.

He can't find his pencil. It's not on the table, it hasn't rolled onto the floor and it's not stuck down the back of the radiator. In a few seconds of stillness, Alex hears a quiet clunk from another room.

The living room is exactly as it was.

His bedroom is undisturbed.

There is not a single item out of place in the bathroom.

Last, he looks over the unused bedroom. There is no furniture in here – no point since nobody sleeps here – but something catches his eye, red on white. His pencil is lying on the windowsill.

"Oh, for crying out loud," he says loud enough for his own voice to soothe his fraying nerves. "Who left that there? Is someone fucking with me?"

He strides over and picks up the pencil.

As he turns to leave, he hears a noise.

One. Quiet. *THUD.*

Alex responds in the way any self-respecting skeptical paranormal researcher would. At least that's what he tells Jaspreet and then Tomas and then Paulina when he calls them one after the other in the hope that their voices might calm him or reassure him with laughter at his expense. The fact that the spare bedroom door is shut tight and the TV is blaring and every light in the house is on is pure coincidence. He asks Jaspreet to find out if the church where the Ozanich funeral was held still exists. To Tomas he delegates checking with the diocese to see if they have any centralized records from that era. Paulina laughs at him until he begins to giggle himself. "Well done, Alex. After years of debunking ghost stories, you actually found a real one."

"That's preposterous. There are no such things as ghosts."

THUMP

Alex starts and shrieks. Paulina's laughter roars out from his phone. "Are you doing this?" Alex demands when his thumping heart and surging adrenaline turn his shock to anger. "Have you put someone up to tormenting the skeptic?"

"No," Paulina says, wheezing a little. "I promise. It's just hilarious to see you rattled for once."

"Glad to be your evening's entertainment." Alex scoffs.

"I'm sorry for laughing at you," Paulina says through bursts of giggles. "Tell you what. To make it up to you, I'll have Oonagh see what she can dig up on Axton from our archives."

"Have her start digitizing the microfiche too," Alex snaps. "It's not 1949 any more."

Alex ends the call and looks round. He's embarrassed at his

reaction to events that he is sure will, in due course, turn out to have been the work of living pranksters. He laughs softly at himself, half expecting Paulina to leap out and show him where the cameras are hidden. He sits down with a fresh cup of tea and his laptop at the kitchen table, puts on a playlist of cheerful 1980s electronica and gets to work on scripting the introduction to his podcast, which he will edit down into his article for Paulina. There are no further disturbances and soon he forgets that he was ever unsettled. When he can barely keep his eyes open, Alex closes his laptop and heads for bed. As he passes the closed door of the vacant bedroom, he pauses and listens.

Silence.

It's silent enough to hear the mains hum from the cables in the walls. Of course it is. There's no one in there.

No one at all.

He darts back into the kitchen, picks up his pad and pencil, strides into the vacant room and leaves them in the middle of the carpet. Then he takes two of his pills and goes to bed feeling a little foolish.

He can tell it's the same place later in the year, or maybe later in the evening. The sunlight slants in from a lower angle, the greens are more muted, and the ground is colder than before. The gurgle and splash of the fountain – he's sure it is a fountain now – sounds louder. Alex pushes himself up to sit and blinks into the sun. "Hello again." The voice sounds warmer this time, more welcoming. "I wondered if you would come back."

Alex peers up but all he can make out is a dark figure, tall and broad, haloed by white sunbeams. He smiles and reaches out his hand. "Help me up, then."

But when the figure's hand reaches for him, the edges blur and soften and fade and Alex sighs into darkness as the dream slips away.

Alex wakes feeling well-rested, as if emerging from a pleasant dream he can't quite remember but looking forward to going back to bed again. He knows the slight fog will disperse and leave his mind clear, so he gets up and showers, makes coffee, checks his email and social media, and reaches for his pencil. That's when he remembers what he did last night before taking his anxiety meds and going to bed. Tutting and frowning at his own silliness, he goes to the unused bedroom to retrieve his pencil and notepad.

They are exactly where he left them. Except the pencil is blunted and the top page is scrawled over and over and over and over.

Dr Griffin. Griffin. GriffinGriffinGriffinGriffin.

Then, at the very bottom, lines broad but faint as if the blunt pencil barely touched the paper: AXTON.

Alex clutches the pad so tightly the paper creaks and crumples between his fingers. The pencil snaps in his fist.

"Griffin," he says out loud.

There's no reply.

"Griffin."

Nothing.

"Griffin!"

Alex's raised voice trembles and squeaks a little, embarrassment warming his cheeks despite his fear. A sudden chill turns his breath into clouds. His hairs prick up and the skin down his back shivers. From all around, Alex feels rather than hears it. A reply, in a quiet but clear voice.

Yes.

"Are you there?" Alex's voice falters, mouth dry. He curses internally at his stupidity. "Paulie, if you're behind this I swear I will—"

The chill lifts. Alex drops the broken halves of his pencil and lets the pad flutter to the floor, suddenly aware that his fingers are aching with the cold and with muscle fatigue from his white-knuckle grip.

He leaves the paper and pencil where they fell and goes back to the warm, bright kitchen, moves his chair so that he faces the door and makes fresh coffee. Frowning, he types in the search box. Doctor Griffin. The screen fills with local medical practices and professional profiles, then a link to the Wikipedia page for The Invisible Man. Alex sighs and rubs his face then tries narrowing the search by adding 1949 to the search box, but that makes it worse. He starts noting down any Dr Griffin who might possibly ever have crossed paths with Henry Strong, but soon it feels like he's swamped with names and dates and addresses. Alex bangs the table with his fist and curses, but a text from Jaspreet makes him hiss out a triumphant *Yesss!* The church mentioned in the newspaper still exists and it is not far away. He replies to ask Jaspreet to meet him there during his lunch break, gets dressed and goes out. A walk in the autumn sunshine might clear his mind.

Jaspreet turns up just after Alex confirms the soot-stained limestone building is locked. They crunch along the neat, gravel path at the front then venture around the side to the small graveyard, overgrown and crowded with lichen-coated stones that stick up higgledy-piggledy like rotting teeth. Alex stops beside one of the last burial plots at the edge of the grounds where a stone wall separates the churchyard from the street. "Jas," he says, fumbling with his camera and snapping a picture. "Look."

Jaspreet jogs over and reads the inscription, letters softened by weathering.

"In Memoriam Harry, much loved son of Greta Ozanich and Henry Strong, born 1st August 1928, died 1949."

Side by side, they give Harry a full minute of respectful silence, then Jaspreet asks, "Wonder what happened to his family?"

"That's easy to find out," a voice behind them says. "All you have to do is ask the right questions of the right person."

Alex whirls round to see a gray-haired woman wearing a black suit with a white clerical collar. Her face is lined with age and her dark eyes are red rimmed and watery, but she cackles and her grin is infectious. "Startled you, didn't I?"

"Yes." Alex smiles back. "I just moved into the–"

She waves her hand. "I know, I know. Eddie Peterson said there was a paranormal investigator on the case. I wondered when you'd show up here to see whose spirit might have been reluctant to pass over, as it were. Come on in, I'm opening up for the morning crowd."

The little church feels even colder and gloomier inside than outside, but dust motes send up cheery sparkles of reflected sunlight from their footsteps. "I'm Sarah," the old woman says. "I took over this parish from my uncle, who knew the Ozanich family personally. There's an old photo of them in here somewhere. I'll find it and show you when I remember where I saw it last."

Alex wants to ask questions but Reverend Sarah doesn't want to answer until they are sitting in the cluttered, musty vestry with cups of tea and a plate of pink wafer biscuits and custard creams. A pendulum clock tick-tocks in the corner although it tells the wrong time. Her face lights up with an unspoken "Ah!" and she takes a book from the shelf beside her, opens it and carefully picks up a photograph, grainy, yellowing and faded at the edges. She slaps the book, pages splayed open, print side down on the desk, oblivious to Jaspreet's look of horror. "This was Father Matthew's library. He said this book and the photo belonged together."

Jaspreet lifts the book, carefully rights it and admires its red cover with gold lettering. "This is a first edition," he says with a hint of excitement and a little reproach. "Worth a fortune, probably. You might have more buried treasure here, reverend. Would you like me to look? Advise you on storage and auctions?"

Sarah reaches across the desk and holds her hand out for the book. "Call me Sarah, please. And thanks, but no. I'm not selling what's not mine."

Alex takes in a sharp breath when he reads the book title as Jaspreet reluctantly hands it over, connections linking vaguely remembered facts. "The Invisible Man! Of course! Doctor Griffin! Sarah, do you know if Harry read this too?"

Sarah only shrugs and pushes the photograph across the desk. "The Ozanichs. My uncle Matthew knew them well enough, although he said they wouldn't talk about Harry after…after what happened."

There's a moment of silence, or perhaps Alex simply tunes out

Sarah's and Jaspreet's voices as the family photograph demands his attention. There's a well-dressed smiling couple in the center, probably Harry's parents. On the left, the young, bearded man in a clerical suit must be Matthew, and a girl of maybe seven or eight holds his hand. And on the right there is a young man, taller than all of them, with dark hair unfashionably long for the era and a serious expression with eyes that seem to pin Alex in place. Alex stares unblinking at the image, trying to recall where he has seen a face like Harry's before, but voices cut through his concentration before he reaches a conclusion.

"That's me," Sarah says, tapping the image of the girl. "The family stayed every summer. I met them although I barely remember it. The year Harry vanished, they–"

"What do you mean, vanished?" Alex leans forward to study the photo again. "There was nothing in the local newspaper. We spent days checking issues from back then."

"Harry's mother, Greta, wanted it kept out of the news. Didn't want gawkers, or opportunists sending ransom notes, or cruel strangers giving them false leads. Matthew took it very badly. He felt responsible for Harry. One of his flock. More than that, actually. Harry loved it here. He wanted to stay on until the end of September, but his parents had to fly home. His folks only agreed to let Harry stay because Father Matthew promised to look after him. Matthew thought it was his fault for not watching the boy better."

"He vanished?" Alex reminds Sarah. She gives him a sharp glare.

"Yes. On his 21st birthday." She takes another pink wafer and crunches it while Alex resists the temptation to yell at her to get on with the story. "Matthew told me Harry was supposed to spend the day studying scripture with him, but he canceled because he had been invited for a tour of the mansion with Mr Axton instead. The whole estate was going up for sale so there wouldn't be another chance to see it in all its glory. Matthew wanted the lad to have a good birthday, so he allowed it. Harry was never seen again."

"Shit!" Jaspreet says, then looks mortified at having sworn in front of the elderly woman. "Sorry. But what a horrible thing to happen. Was he…how was his body found?"

"Well," Sarah says with a deep sigh, "officially, in the grounds. Officially, on his way back from the mansion he fell and hit his head. Officially, he rolled into a ditch and was missed by the search party. A dog-walker found remains three months later on All Saints' Day."

"And unofficially?" Alex leans forward, elbow resting on Sarah's desk.

Sarah raises an eyebrow at him. "Unofficially, although that grave contains human remains, I have no idea whose they are."

Alex stares at her. "Surely someone would have noticed! Or checked!"

The reverend shrugs. "Not necessarily. I mean nowadays, yes, there's DNA and all sorts. But then? Police found a badly-decomposed body in stagnant water. A doctor said what was left of the remains matched the description of the missing person as well as could be expected. An open casket," she says dryly, "was discouraged. Besides, the boy's mother said she felt it in her heart her son was gone." Sarah frowns. "No, that isn't quite right. She said he was lost. Matthew tried to find out what might have happened to Harry, but he got nowhere."

"The dates can't be right," Jaspreet adds. "Missing for three months! How could he not have been found? What about getting a DNA test done now?"

"So maybe the story is inaccurate in places," Sarah snaps, looking unimpressed. "I'm telling it second-hand from someone who didn't want to talk about it fifty years ago. And whose DNA are the police going to compare it with? Harry has no living relatives to demand a test like that. Or to pay for it."

"Thank you," Alex says, jumping in to prevent any further friction. "I appreciate anything you can tell us."

Sarah gives Alex a curt nod and looks up as the door opens and another elderly woman looks in, apologizing for disturbing them. Sarah's face lights up. "Lily! Thanks for coming." Sarah looks back at Alex. "Sorry. I remember almost nothing of the family myself. I was too young really, but I liked them. That's all I can tell you. I went back to school and Harry's parents came to stay with Uncle Matthew for a few weeks then returned to America."

Alex and Jaspreet thank Sarah, nod politely at Lily, then leave, promising to keep Sarah updated on the investigation. "There won't be any birth or death records for the parents, then," Alex says as they walk away from the little church building. "Not locally anyway."

"But there should be a death certificate for Harry," Jaspreet replies.

Alex nods. "So we can confirm the official story." He checks his watch. "Should be open by the time we get into town. Do you have to get back to work right away?"

Jaspreet pulls a face until Alex offers to buy him sandwiches, but he makes a show of checking the time and shakes his head.

The receptionist at the registrar's office tells Alex politely that he ought to go home, register online, and use the searchable database. It's such obvious advice that he smiles at his own expectation that, like the local paper and the local diocese, local government would be stuck in 1949. When he gets home, he writes up all he can remember of Sarah's story. Then he signs up online to access the register and finds Harry's death certificate. It is a digitized copy of the handwritten original. The pixelated writing is a challenge, but it lists Henry Ozanich-Strong as 21 years old. Place of death lists only the name of the estate. The date and time of death are listed as unknown, as is the cause of death. The coroner's signature is illegible.

Alex yells in frustration. He walks into the vacant bedroom. "Who the fuck are you and what the fuck happened to you!" He stands stock still, fists clenched by his sides. "It feels like the more I dig the less I know. And now I'm yelling at a ghost – who definitely does not exist – in an empty room!"

There's no chill in the air. Nothing to make Alex's skin tingle. Sunlight streams in through the window and shows up stains on the carpet. Alex sighs. "What am I even doing? A stupid story got me freaked out. I suppose I should talk to Peterson and see if I can visit old man Axton."

The temperature falls so quickly the chill paralyzes Alex's lungs for a few seconds and his vision mists. All the moisture in the air condenses and freezes and falls as white dust. He coughs and covers his mouth and nose with his sleeve as if to warm the air going in. The cold pinches his nose and ears and stabs at his throat. The bedroom door slams shut with a sharp bang. Condensation mists the windows, freezes into sparkles and blocks the warmth of the sun. Fear gnaws at Alex's bowels and blood rushes in his ears.

THUD…

THUD.

Alex turns, wrenches the door open and runs. He doesn't stop until he's halfway up the crazy paving path outside his house.

He's still listening to the buzzing of his own ears and shivering although the autumn sunshine is enough to warm him through. He realizes his phone is vibrating in his pocket. "Hi." He takes a breath. "Paulie?"

"Yes, sweetie. Buy me dinner and I'll tell you what Oonagh found."

"Uh, sure. Yes, if I can put dinner on expenses."

Paulina gives a short, sharp laugh as permission, then replies, "You okay? You sound weird."

"I'm fine."

"Seven?"

Paulina suggests a cheap and cheerful restaurant. Alex agrees. He turns to go back indoors, feeling silly now he's spoken to Paulie. He studies his perfectly ordinary house. The living room and kitchen windows look welcoming again, blinds half down, with the front door between like two lidded eyes over a sharp nose. Movement catches his eye and he squints against the low November sun that hasn't quite dipped below the roof line. For just a fleeting instant, he's sure there is someone looking out of the kitchen window at him. He blinks and they're gone.

"Good afternoon!"

Alex turns at the call. It's Peterson. Alex looks at his kitchen window again and laughs. "Hi. I saw your reflection and for a minute I thought there was someone in my house. Spooked me."

"Spooked the ghost hunter?" Peterson smiles. "Surely not. I was going to call. Axton's nursing staff have been having a hell of a time. Apparently he's all riled up about something. Keeps throwing things and yelling."

"Oh?" Alex tries to display only casual interest. He points towards his front door. "Would you like to have a cup of coffee and tell me about it?"

Peterson laughs and shakes his head. "Thanks but no. I'm not setting foot in that house."

Alex lets his smile falter. "Well then. What is old man Axton yelling about?"

"Nobody knows." Peterson shrugs. "Between them, his specialist carers are experts in a dozen medical disciplines. But none of them can explain why he keeps yelling for 'Dr Griffin.' His gerontologist is Dr Finch."

Alex opens and closes his mouth a couple of times, but no sound comes out. Peterson doesn't seem to notice, bids him good afternoon and leaves. After a minute of searching for shadows in the windows, Alex goes inside. "All right," he says opening every door. "I am willing to keep an open mind about Harry Ozanich-Strong and whatever the name Griffin means to you. I don't think you mean me any harm, but–"

THUD THUD

"–but I need answers. Was that two for no you don't mean me any harm or two for no I'm wrong?"

Silence.

"Okay. One for yes you intend to hurt me. Two for no you do not intend to hurt me. Three for you have not decided yet."

THUD THUD

"You could be lying."

THUD THUD THUD

"That's not fucking funny, Griffin."

No response.

"Why don't you want me to see Axton?"

No response.

Alex bites his lip. "This yes-no thing is tiresome. I'm going out. I need to think."

Alex grabs his keys, his coat and his laptop, and leaves. He finds a cafe in town and sips fancy coffee, tuning out the background chatter while he mulls over his notes. He searches 'communicating with ghosts' and snorts at the sites he's directed to since he has already debunked several of them as frauds. Next, he tries filtering out the more clickbait-y results, and the ones he knows are bogus, and the ones that claim to tell the future, and the ones promoting miracle cures, and the ones based overseas, and the ones promoting love spells. There is not much left. One, in fact. There's a plain web page and a phone number. It rings out then goes to voicemail when he calls back. "Hi," Alex says after the beep. "Marion Kirper? I think I need your help."

He doesn't expect a reply so he's not disappointed when his phone doesn't ring. Paulina is waiting for him at the restaurant and greets him with a pearly smile and a brusque, perfumed hug. They are given a table for two and they smile at the staff who clearly think they are on a date. Once they have ordered, Paulina leans forwards. "This Axton fellow was a piece of work."

Alex leans forward too. "Really?"

Paulina holds Alex's gaze and nods slowly. "Oonagh said he was into some dodgy stuff, apparently. Black marketeer during the war. Got off with a fine on account of having enough money to pay it. In the thirties an Axton was accused of witchcraft and necromancy but of course nobody took that shit seriously even then." Alex raises his eyebrows. "I know!" Paulina laughs. "Prime candidate for your investigations. Even further back, in 1912, someone called Axton was implicated in a disappearance."

Alex can't lean any further forward without bumping foreheads with Paulina. There's a cough beside them and Paulina leans back. Two plates of pasta are slid onto their placemats and a server waits with a parmesan grater, a pepper grinder, and a smile. Alex waits until they are alone again. "Tell me about that."

"Nothing came of it. A lad disappeared. Twenty-four years old. Axton was suspected of being involved but there was no evidence. The police report was brief and deferential."

"Someone got paid off?"

Paulina shrugs. "Apparently, the lad had a girlfriend his folks didn't approve of. The report says the boy eloped, got married, and boarded a ship in Liverpool under a different name, with his new wife. He was old enough, so the case was dropped a week after it was opened. It's a wonder there was any record of it at all."

Alex eats a few mouthfuls then pauses to tell Paulina what he found out over the course of the day, omitting the parts where he actually spoke to the possible-but-impossible ghost of Harry Ozanich-Strong, because he's not sure he believes it himself. Paulina's nose almost twitches at the story.

"Disappeared? Twenty-one years old?"

"It's probably a coincidence," Alex warns. "I can understand why some people want to make a break for freedom. Maybe the lad did elope in 1912. Maybe this Ozanich guy ran away for a few weeks in 1949 and had an unfortunate accident."

"Maybe. I'll have Oonagh keep looking if we're not too busy. She likes investigating."

"Thanks." Alex leans back at last.

When Alex gets home, the streetlights are fog-haloed, and the cold has a sharp clarity about it. He is just turning onto his footpath when he sees a small figure waiting by his door. "Can I help you?"

"No," a voice muffled by scarves replies. "But I can help you, Alexander. You called me."

Alex opens the door and ushers Marion inside. He puts on all the lights. Marion gives a knowing laugh. "Get the kettle on," she says, shaking out peroxide curls and wiping mist from her glasses with her headscarf. "I'm chilled to the bones. Came as soon as I got your message."

Alex frowns. "Did I leave you my address?"

Marion gives him a withering look. "Even us psychics use the internet sometimes. I like your podcast. Especially the episodes where you debunk fakes."

Marion walks from room to room. She comes into the kitchen just as the tea is ready. "You have a presence. Not evil, but not settled."

"Oh? The usual unfinished business thing?"

Marion snorts scornfully. "Don't assume that I'm one of those cold-reading charlatans who give genuine mediums like me a bad name. You know as well as I do that the unfinished business line is bullshit. Some souls just want to hang around. Delay the inevitable."

"The inevitable judgment and heaven or hell?" Alex asks with a sneer.

"The inevitable decay into nothingness. This one is strong." Marion slurps her tea and Alex suppresses a shudder. "Maybe if you solve his murder he'll leave. Maybe he won't."

"Wait," Alex says slowly. "Murder?"

Marion nods. "Without a doubt. I feel his desperation. And his fear. He knew his end was coming and he couldn't avoid it. He wasn't ready to go. So he's staying, grasping on to every thread that connects him to this existence."

"And?" Alex frowns. "That's still a variation on the standard unfinished business story. But why here? Why haunt a fifties bungalow? He couldn't have died in it. It wasn't built yet."

"Don't throw the baby out with the bathwater, Alexander." Marion holds her mug out. Alex refills it. "I wonder." She pauses to suck in a mouthful of tea and swallow it. "What was here before?"

"Part of Axton's gardens, I expect."

"You expect, but you don't know. Huh." Marion looks up at Alex in a way that makes him feel like he's being scolded. "Come on then, Alexander. Let's see if your unsettled soul wants to talk."

Alex gets up to lead Marion into the unused bedroom, but

Marion is ahead of him. She tells Alex to bring her a chair. He carries through a dining chair and a cushion, and Marion gets as comfortable as she can, then announces, "I can wait until you're ready."

"Oh then I'll—"

"Not you." Alex's face warms, and he lurks by the door. "Stay. I expect he'll want to talk to you. He has tried, hasn't he?"

Alex nods. "The one knock for yes, two for no thing. And he wrote a name down."

THUD

Marion laughs. "So I see. Hello…" She cocks her head. "Griffin."

"Who is Griffin?" Alex blurts out. "I thought Harry Ozanich-Strong was the ghost."

"Hush. The energy around this one is fickle. That's the name he calls himself."

Alex bites his lip. He stands silent for so long he wonders if he ought to fetch a chair for himself too. Marion looks up after a few more minutes. "Harry Ozanich-Strong died in 1949."

"I know. I saw the notice in the newspaper, the grave and the death certificate."

"And Griffin came into existence."

Alex frowns. "I don't understand."

Marion shushes him with a gesture. "Axton," she says, and the door rattles on its hinges. The cold slithers down Alex's spine again. "You can feel his anger, his hatred, yes?" Alex nods. Marion's eyes close. "And his fear." The rattling stops and the cold lifts abruptly. Marion shivers and rubs her arms. "He means you no harm. He likes you."

"He likes me?" Alex's eyebrows rise. "I debunk ghost stories for a living."

"Maybe that's why. You're still here. You're not going to run in terror if he gets restless. At least," she adds, smirking. "You won't run far."

Alex remembers earlier that day running out of his own house and seeing the dim shadow of a figure looking out at him from the kitchen window. "Was he making fun of me?"

Marion just smiles. "Come on. I can teach you a way of making contact with this Griffin. Is there more tea?"

Alex makes a fresh pot. Marion looks at him thoughtfully from the doorway. "I don't suppose you have any…no. No you probably wouldn't."

"Any what?"

"Well, certain herbs are known for opening the mind a little wider. It eases communication."

Alex looks in his cupboard. "Dried oregano? Thyme?"

Marion gives an amused shake of her head. Alex realizes what she means, and he laughs. "None of that, sorry. Messes with my medication."

"Oh?" she perks up. "Anything psychoactive?"

"Anxiety medication." Alex shakes the half-finished blister pack in front of Marion. She takes it from him and looks at the name.

"Take a low dose," Marion says decisively. "It will help."

Alex takes one pill, the lowest dose he uses when he just needs to take the edge off a difficult day. They drink tea quietly for twenty minutes, then Marion tells Alex to bring another chair to the empty bedroom and get comfortable. After half an hour of 'clear your mind' and 'concentrate on the here and now' Alex's head nods and jerks. Marion pats his arm as she gets up. "That will do for now. Your barriers are weakening. Keep trying."

When Marion has gone, Alex goes back into the unused bedroom and sits on one of the chairs.

"I think you can hear me. And I heard you too, one time. Maybe twice. But I'm tired. Goodnight, Griffin." This time as he walks through the door, he's almost sure he hears a whispered *goodnight*. "Since you're listening, I want to know what happened to Harry on his 21st birthday, and what Axton has to do with it. I won't visit Axton since you have made your opinion clear. But my friend Paulina told me a few things about him. Maybe…maybe you… maybe Harry wasn't his first victim." Alex waits but there is no response. No chill, no slamming door, no knocking. "Well then, goodnight again."

He takes two more pills to make sure he sleeps through the night and goes to bed.

He doesn't question the childish, crayon-yellow sun so high in a cornflower sky, with puffy white clouds he could almost reach out and touch, and distant hazy wisps so high up they blur gray into the blue. It's warm and he's happy. He's in a garden filled with an eruption of flowers in pinks and reds and lilacs to the point of being overgrown, and there is a heady fragrance of honeysuckle and rose. Behind him, water splashes merrily. "I was here," a voice says beside him. "I liked this spot. I'd bring a book and sit with my back to the fountain and read for hours."

Alex turns to look at the owner of the voice. A young man stands there, lit by the sunlight. Broad shoulders, hands on hips, tall. Alex takes in his dark wavy hair and intense brown eyes. The man parts wide lips to reveal uneven, white teeth. "This was all supposed to be mine one day, he said."

Alex feels his brow crinkle into a frown. "What do you mean?"

"The Axton inheritance. He promised it to me. All I had to do was visit him every year on my birthday. I insisted we come here on vacation every summer. He kept promising and then delaying. Another year. Another year. He told me I was special. Chosen. Born for greater things than my parents could provide. That I'd be a failure if I refused his offer to tutor me about how the world works."

Alex feels his blood run cold. "Harry—"

"Griffin, please." Soft features harden. "Harry is gone. I had to lose him to survive."

"But surely you are—"

"Harry was a boy, afraid. Griffin is stronger. Griffin fought back and hid."

"Griffin."

Griffin nods. "Harry could not endure Axton's demands. Harry's lost and Griffin is here in his place."

"What–" Alex swallows, stomach churning. "What happened here, Griffin? Can you tell me? What happened to Harry?"

Griffin nods once. "Better. I'll show you."

Alex feels his head swim like he's going to faint, although he knows on some level at least that he is dreaming. He sees the gardens in the full bloom of late summer instead of the muted greens, browns and golds of a damp autumn. It feels wrong, like he's looking down from an unfamiliar angle. His hands, when he holds them out for balance at the sudden lurch in his senses, are broader than they should be, with pale skin tanned darker than his own pallid white. With wonder, he realizes that he's looking out through someone else's eyes. Griffin's eyes.

"I was reading in this garden," Griffin's voice says softly inside his head, "when he called me to go inside."

Sure enough, a man who might be any age between forty and seventy smiles and waves from the terrace above the splashing fountain. Alex squints against the sunlight but the man remains just out of focus, as if Griffin's memory doesn't want him to look too closely. He walks towards the terrace and climbs the steps, following the man's back as he opens a set of glass doors and waits for Griffin to catch up.

"Is that Ax–"

"Don't say it. Yes. It's him."

Alex watches like a passenger in the front seat of a car as Griffin plays out his memory. He follows Axton inside, eyes adjusting to the gloom as the older man leads the way through the garden room into the passageway beyond.

Axton's head turns and his smile widens, stretched lips over off-white teeth. Alex senses Griffin's revulsion. "I expect you'd like the full tour before the builders come in to ruin my family heritage, eh?"

"Thank you, sir," Griffin's reply comes from inside Alex's head. "I appreciate you taking the trouble to show me around."

Axton's smile looks predatory. Alex shudders. "It's my pleasure."

Axton pauses at a narrow paneled door set into the wall under the staircase. It's a servants' door, so cleverly made that a passing glance would miss it.

Axton opens the door, a smooth click without a creak. "I made a promise that you would be part of my inheritance, and I intend to make good on that promise very soon. So, I ought to show you what you will be getting. Shall we start at the bottom and work our way up?"

Emotions surge in Alex's dream. He feels Harry pulled on by anticipation and perhaps a little greed, hope that he is about to become rich enough to travel on his own and begin a career writing about his experiences. He feels Griffin's fear and despair pulling at him, urging him to turn and run, and he wonders what would happen if he did simply turn his dream-self around and walk away.

But he can't. He can't change this sequence of events, because it has already happened and he cannot change the course of someone else's nightmare.

Alex steps through the door into a short passageway ending at a staircase that spirals into darkness. His feet feel their way down, hand gripping the cold, metal rail, until Axton laughs and, with a buzz and a flicker, a dim, yellow light comes on. In Alex's head, Harry laughs. Griffin is silent, as if holding his breath.

"Through there." Axton points over Alex's shoulder at a rough, plain, wooden door. "That is where we will begin."

Alex pushes the door open.

Axton shoves Alex hard in the middle of his back and he stumbles forward into the room. In the poor light that splashes in from the electric lights in the servants' passage, Alex sees geometric drawings in black paint or tar, stark black lines on the pale limestone floor. He falls to his knees.

He's kneeling in the center of the room.

And he can't move.

Behind him, Axton laughs, low and breathy. "I promised you would be part of my inheritance. If you misinterpreted that to mean that your life would be made easier at the expense of mine, then that is hardly my fault. Feeding your avarice was so easy it was barely any fun."

Alex feels Harry's alarm spike. His heart is racing and his joints feel like overwound springs ready to release, but he's as helpless as a rabbit in a snare. There's something at the edge of his vision, a bundle in the corner lit by light leaking in through the doorway. He realizes with a scream he can't voice that it is a shriveled and shrunken human form in fetal position.

Axton pulls him over onto his back then kneels at his side. "It wasn't all lies," he says to Harry's supine form while nodding towards the pile of remains. "You will live here in my house. But you'll become part of me just like he did."

Axton rips open Harry's shirt and presses one cold hand to his chest, then begins to chant.

Alex jerks awake with a yell and sits up. He's breathing hard, sweating and dizzy and filled with a fading sense of terror as if from a nightmare just on the point of slipping from his memory. "Harry!" he calls out, voice loud and desperate in the empty house. "Griffin!" As his breathing and his heartbeat calm, he murmurs, "Oh, god," and reaches for his phone but it's in the kitchen so he has to get up. It's not light outside yet and the sleeping pills have not completely worn off. He stumbles through the house, snaps on the kitchen light and calls Paulina. "I know," he says through Paulina's cursing. "About Axton."

He talks as if he's afraid he'll forget.

In truth, he wishes he could. Paulina asks him to repeat what he says. When he runs out of new words to say, she asks how he found out. Alex is stumped for a few seconds then admits, "Griffin told me."

"I see," Paulina says after an embarrassing silence. "So how much medication did you take?"

"Paulie, you know how skeptical I am. You know I am the least likely person in the world to fall for a haunting scam. You know me, Paulina." Alex is trembling. He walks into the unused bedroom and sits on one of the dining chairs. "Paulie, you don't have to believe me, but you owe me the benefit of the doubt. Just until we do some more digging on…on you know who."

"Fine." Paulina sounds doubtful. "I'll get Oonagh back in the archive. And you need to promise to see your doctor."

"Okay, I will. I promise. Thanks." Alex ends the call and takes a deep breath. "Well. She'll help get to the bottom of this. Thinks I'm actually losing my grip on reality – hah, she might be right – but she will help. Can I talk to Marion about this?"

There's the suggestion of a sigh, and one soft *THUD*.

Alex leaves the room, showers, dresses, drinks coffee. He calls Marion and leaves a message. He feels out of sorts all morning, like there's a vague wrongness about the day, and he flits from trying to write to trying to read to trying to watch TV. Nothing holds his attention. "I need to go out," he announces to the empty house. "Clear my head."

The weather is murky and fallen leaves, wet with rain, slick the pavement. Alex walks through November drizzle into town, where he sets up at a cafe and sends Marion a text in case she plans to pay him another surprise home visit. At least he can watch people scurry past the plate glass window beside his table when he can't focus on reading or writing. He whiles away a couple of hours with tea and distractions until the chair opposite him is pulled back and the scrape makes him jerk his head up. A slim, dark-haired woman rests her hand on the back of the chair until Alex nods. She sits and clasps her hands, purses her lips, while deciding what to say. "I saw you from outside," Oonagh says after a few seconds. "I have some information for you, but…not here. Can you come to the offices? Paulina's going wild. She's going to want your sources. Confidentially, of course."

Alex nods and sighs. "That will be tricky," he says. "I don't think my sources are going to be in a position to stand up to scrutiny."

"Shame." Oonagh's face twists in disgust. "I don't care how old or infirm he is. If he killed someone, he should be in jail."

Alex nods. "So, you found out more?"

Oonagh tenses, caged fingers going white at the knuckles for a second. "Come to the office, Alex. I'll tell Paulie you're on your way."

Alex nods and a thought strikes him. "Hey, would the paper have plans for the original grounds of the estate, and for the housing development?"

Oonagh raises her eyebrows in surprise. "I suppose we might have an aerial photo of the building site. It was a popular news topic back then: penniless nobs losing their land and us plebs getting decent housing on it instead. People wanted to see progress." Oonagh gets up and smiles. "I'll see what I can dig up when I have time. Have you had no luck finding it on the internet?"

Alex rolls his eyes. "I tried that already."

As soon as Oonagh has waved goodbye through the window, he types the name of his housing estate into the internet search box. He finds a grainy aerial shot of the estate with the grounds overgrown and a few dirt roads encroaching on the boundary walls. He identifies where he was standing in his dream when he saw Griffin. There's a perfect circle that could be the dried-up fountain he remembers gushing behind him, and trees that could be the orchard in front. When he thinks he has his position pinpointed, he screenshots the photo and marks his dream location with a rough oval. Next, he uses his maps app in satellite mode to see the housing estate as it is now. He screenshots this too.

He knows what he's going to find before he sees it. When he adjusts the scale and rotation of both photos and overlays the ghost of the old on the new, the oval he drew intersects the back corner of his house. Alex reaches for his tea and is surprised to find it's cold. He packs his laptop away and leaves the cafe. He checks the time on his phone and sees a message from Marion that makes him blush (yes Griffin was handsome but that is not important), then walks quickly to the newspaper office. Paulina waves him through immediately.

"Psychic connection? Strangely realistic dream?" She sighs and

glares at Alex. "It won't do, you know. This story will go national."
She sighs again. "I want to publish something that'll stand up on
its own if anyone tries to sue us for defamation."

"Paulina, if I had a concrete source, I would hand them over."
Alex grips his knees. "You know that. I trust you."

"All we have right now is a collection of disappearances that
are tenuously linked to the estate and the word of a man high on
sleeping pills." She leans forward. "It won't do, Alexander."

"Well, what do you suggest? I wish I could tell you Harry
Ozanich-Strong walked into my house, alive and well at over ninety
years old, and gave me a witness statement."

They glare at each other for ten awkward seconds. "All right,"
Paulina says. "Oonagh?"

Oonagh brings out a laptop and opens it at the conference
table. She connects the projector and closes the blinds so that the
three of them are cocooned in semi-darkness.

"1912," Oonagh says. "George Archer, 24, vanishes after visiting
Axton to do repairs. Never seen again. 1923. Henry Denton, 22,
vanishes after visiting Axton to attend to an injured horse. Found
three weeks later, what was left of him, in a ditch just beyond
the estate boundary wall." Alex half listens to dates and names
until Oonagh gets to the one he knows is coming. "1949. Henry
Ozanich-Strong, known as Harry, 21–"

"Stop." Alex clenches both fists. "That has got to be enough,"
he adds quietly.

"No." Paulina shakes her head. "It's a lot of coincidence. I can't
even call it evidence, Alex. There's nothing that links Axton directly
to any of these disappearances."

"So…so we leave it?" Alex feels his voice shake. "He gets away
with it? No. No, that can't happen. Paulie, I saw what happened to
Harry. To all of them. They're saying Axton is acting up, shouting…
what if he's getting ready again? How long before someone else
vanishes? Maybe a cleaner or a student away from home or a locum
nurse from outside the area. Someone who won't be missed right
away. We have to do something!"

"Hush, Alex. We need evidence. Maybe someone saw something. I can sit on this for now, ready to publish the instant we have anything solid." Paulina squeezes Alex's hand. "This is too big to let go. Oonagh, who do we know who fits the profile?"

Oonagh raises her eyebrows. "You want to send someone in?"

Alex stares from one to the other, aghast. "Tell me you are not sending someone as bait to that monster. I…I can't tell you who my source is *but I believe him.*"

"Of course not." Paulina shakes her head. "That would be unethical."

Paulina and Oonagh exchange a glance that Alex almost misses. "Don't do it," he pleads. "What will happen, do you think? Journalism intern vanishes. You want that on your hands? I won't be part of it."

Alex goes home. He's raging and shaking, and he takes his medication just so he can settle enough to think one thought at a time. He paces the house talking aloud to Griffin until he feels a little drowsy, then he sits in the kitchen. "I don't know what to do, Griffin."

But I do, comes the reply, clear in Alex's head.

Alex looks around. There is a suggestion of a shadow by the window. He can see through it to the trees outside, but it is definitely there. "Griffin?"

Yes.

"That's you, by the window?"

Yes.

"Am I hallucinating?"

Alex hears a soft laugh and the sound of a coffee mug banging on the worktop twice.

He wakes up an hour later with his head throbbing and a crick in his neck from falling asleep at the kitchen table. With a soft curse falling from his lips, he gets up and staggers to bed to sleep it off. He dreams of a dinner with Griffin and an older couple, smiling and laughing.

He dreams of a day exploring the grounds of the mansion, hand in hand with a dark-haired boy whose eyes shine with the excitement of finding a walled garden and the cut-back stumps outlining what was once a beech maze.

He dreams of pulling the boy to his side behind a gnarly old yew tree and kissing him.

The boy – man – Griffin looks at him in surprise. Alex is on the point of apologizing when Griffin grins at him and cups his face, then kisses him in return. Alex feels every muscle under his control relax. Griffin's kiss is soft, hesitant even, and he pulls back before Alex is ready to stop. "Griffin," he says, a hand coming up to touch Griffin's soft hair.

"Is this what you want?" Griffin asks.

"Only if you want it too."

Griffin smiles and leans in to kiss Alex again. Alex feels the rough bark of the tree against his back, the texture of Griffin's hair between his fingers and the soft warmth of Griffin's lips on his. There is a nagging feeling this is not possible, not real, but it doesn't seem important right now. Griffin's weight is pressing against him, pushing him back against the tree. He's hard and uncomfortable in his trousers, so Griffin pops the button and pulls the zipper down. Alex slides one hand from Griffin's hair down to his waistband and unfastens his trousers too. A cool hand slips into his shorts. Alex cups Griffin then strokes, murmuring "yes" to Griffin's unspoken question. The rough bark of the trunk behind him becomes softer and his head is spinning and he's coming and–

–and he wakes up in bed, a cry of Griffin's name still in the air and come cooling on his shirt. He lies there for a minute, mulling over his dream – of course it was a dream, nothing more. Still, he thinks, there's no harm in trying to get it back. Alex closes his eyes and concentrates on remembering the dream-feeling of Griffin's mouth on his and Griffin's body pressing him against the tree.

"Hello," Griffin says. "My turn?"

Alex's heart beats harder. Griffin is there.

No, that's not right. Alex knows he is still lying on top of his bed, eyes closed, only the weight of his clothes on him. He's warm and the covers are soft under him. There's no gnarled old tree with bark that digs into his shoulders and no yellow sunlight filtering through green leaves to dapple Griffin's face.

Griffin is *here*. Alex's eyelids flutter. "Don't!" Griffin's voice is in his head. He keeps his eyes closed. "Don't break the dream."

"Is this a dream?"

He senses Griffin's amusement. "Perhaps. You like it?"

"Yes." In his bed, a weight settles, warm on his body, and soft lips kiss his. He wraps his arms around Griffin's waist, parts his lips for the kiss. Griffin rolls his hips and Alex giggles. "Impatient!"

Griffin pulls back. "I waited a long time. Eyes closed!"

"I want to look at you. With my eyes, not my head."

"Not yet."

Alex smiles and slides his hands over the swell of Griffin's backside. "All right."

Griffin's waistband is still loose from before or perhaps, Alex thinks, that's just how he remembered it in his dream. Griffin raises his hips enough for Alex to move one hand around the front.

Alex sniggers. "Might have known I'd dream of my perfect man."

Griffin laughs. "Thanks, I think. Hope I meet expectations."

Alex reaches up blindly for another kiss and meets those soft lips again. Griffin shifts, thrusts into his hand, and moans quietly against his mouth. "I want to see you," Alex asks again. "Let me see you."

"Not yet. Just this. Alex. Aah."

It only takes a minute or two before Griffin is crying out Alex's name and coming. Griffin collapses onto Alex and nuzzles at his neck. "I'll be gone when you wake yourself up."

"Then I'll stay asleep." But he knows it's impossible and the warm weight of Griffin on him is already lifting. "Ah, not yet," he sighs, but Griffin fades into wisps of memory, leaving only the faintest impression of a kiss under his ear.

When Alex opens his eyes he's alone. It can't be late because it's still light outside. He gets up, peels off his soiled shirt, puts on a clean one, fixes his trousers then wanders into the kitchen. He puts a frozen pizza in the oven and idly taps at his laptop while it cooks. "Griffin knows what to do," he murmurs. There's no shadowy presence, no voice in his head, just the vaguely reassuring feeling that he's not alone.

There's a missed call on his phone so he taps the name. When it connects, Paulina's words gush out. "Alex, you'll never believe what Oonagh found. Disappearances around that estate going way back. Wa-a-ay before the newspaper started. She's got a friend in the local history group. I'll text you her number. Call her. Tell me right away if she has anything more than coincidence."

The person is Marion Kirper.

He calls, and this time Marion answers on the first ring. She's in his vacant bedroom slurping tea forty minutes later. "You made contact," she observes, a hint of a smirk on her lips.

"I..." Alex sighs. "I don't know what to call it. Hallucination? Lucid dreaming?"

"You made contact," Marion repeats more firmly, breath condensing in the chill. "He won't speak to me today. He's resting. It must have cost him a lot to appear to you like that. He's still drawing energy."

Alex looks at Marion's neutral expression. With a flush of embarrassment, he wonders if she knows more about the nature of how Griffin 'made contact' than she's letting on. "Griffin said he knows what to do. About—" He stops short of saying the name that clearly upsets Griffin so much. "Kitchen's warmer," he says instead. Marion nods and they take their mugs back to the cozy kitchen.

"I can't shed any light on what Griffin thinks he can do," Marion says. "Old you-know-who has been a personal project of mine for a long time. Ever since..." She sips her tea. "Since someone close to me went missing and suddenly it wasn't all just rumors and folk tales about young men vanishing any more."

"Paulina has an investigator on the case. Oonagh is very thorough. If there's solid evidence, she'll unearth it."

Marion glares at him. "You think I've not already found out everything solid there is to know? Not that the police take my kind seriously."

Alex shrugs. "I'm not saying anything. I mean… Look, maybe if you and Oonagh share what you know something will connect. Maybe Griffin can tell me more. Maybe it will all fit together, and we can…"

"What, Alexander? What can we do?"

"Paulina wants him on trial and in jail."

"I know more than she does. Even I know that he'll be untouchable with a steady supply of young offenders who will be written off as victims of drugs, fights, or suicides."

Alex can't meet Marion's wrinkled eyes. "I see your point. That won't do at all."

"And what about you," Marion says quietly. "What do you want?"

"For what he's done?" Alex sits back. He puts his mug on the table and clasps his hands around it. He holds Marion's steady gaze. "I want him dead."

"Too bad. I think he already is."

All Alex can offer is frowning confusion. Marion sighs. "Oh, come on. Use your brain for once. Oonagh probably found that the first record of him owning the land you now live on was in 1802. He was an adult then, and an old one. How can he still be alive?" She waits but Alex has no answer that makes any sense. "He's not. And he has not been, at least as we understand it, for at least that long. Maybe longer. I bet she's found no birth or death records. That's not suspicious on its own. Wars, bombs, fires, you know? Maybe the man we know of is a descendant who took an ancestor's identity. But even then there are no records of him as a child or a young man. Say he is one hundred years old. You'd expect someone born even back then to have records of birth or entry to the country. Passport. Primary school roll. Call-up papers or a record of exemption from military service. Medical records. Something should have survived. But I bet you that there is nothing. As far as I can tell he has always existed, always here, and he has adapted as the world changed around him." Marion sits back and sighs. "So, tell me, Alexander. How do you kill a being who shouldn't be alive?"

The answer slides into his head so quietly that the thought startles him when it coalesces into words in Griffin's welcome voice.

With someone who has no life to lose.

As the wintry nights stretch out and frost sparkles the mornings, Alex only occasionally feels like he's not alone in his house. He claims the master bedroom as his own and turns the smaller room into a study where he can work on his podcast and sporadic, paid writing projects, and turns the heating up in both. When anxiety keeps him from sleep, his small-hours mind churning over and over the unimportant minutiae of the day, he takes his medication and Griffin flits in and out of his dreams to smile and kiss him and tell him to be patient. The vision of the tall, dark-haired man never stays more than a few seconds. Despite the longing he feels, Alex wakes with a smile.

He gets a call while he's perusing Christmas trees in the outdoor market, and he fumbles his phone, fingers stiff with cold. "Paulina?"

"Alex. Can you come to the office? There's been a… development."

Alex's stomach flutters and he feels light-headed. "What kind of development?"

"Just get here. Come right in. Front desk knows you're on your way."

He pushes the blue spruce he'd picked out back into the pile and runs.

Alex is waved through reception as soon as he arrives. Around a small conference table sit Paulina, Oonagh and Marion. After a few minutes of awkward silence, the Reverend Sarah fills one of the final two seats. Jaspreet, there out of curiosity about Alex's inability to debunk this haunting, arrives with coffee and claims the last seat.

"All right," Paulina says. "Tomas – he's our researcher," she tells the reverend, "just sent a report." Alex frowns. Paulina won't meet his eye. "As some of you know, I gave Tomas the task of infiltrating the care home."

Alex's cup rattles when he puts it down. "You sent someone in there? After all you know about Axton?"

Paulina sighs. "I don't really 'know' anything. Tomas has the right background, and he looks the part."

"You mean he's a thirty-year-old med school dropout who looks twenty," Alex snaps. "It's irresponsible–"

"Plus," Paulina says, raising her voice just enough and glaring at Alex. "He went in there without any pressure from me. He volunteered for it." She taps her laptop. "His report."

The projector shows images from Tomas's button camera inside the mansion, while Paulina narrates and Oonagh chimes in now and then with extra information. There are medical staff in teal scrubs going about their duties. Figures in white occasionally flit by and there are glimpses of staff in gaudy red. Paulina pauses the slideshow. "Those red scrubs are Axton's private staff. They're mostly separate from the other medical and support staff but they share facilities. Watch."

The next slide has a low-res, muffled video. "Hi, mind if I sit here?"

Tomas's voice comes through louder then the rest and Alex has to concentrate to hear the replies.

"Sure, help yourself. New here?"

"Yeah, started a couple of weeks ago. So, what do I have to do to get a cute red uniform like yours?" The other person laughs. "I mean it. You guys are the elite, so I heard."

"Do yourself a favor, love–oh, good afternoon, sir. This is…"

"Tom. I'm new."

"This is Tom. Tom, this is Dr Finch. My boss."

"Pleased to meet you, Dr Finch." The scene judders as Tomas gets up and shakes hands with the doctor in the red coat. "I hope you don't mind, sir. I was asking your colleague here how to get promoted to your team. I'm new and I'm still finding my feet but I want to make a good career for myself."

"I see." Dr Finch looks silently at Tomas for a few seconds. "Is this your first job, son?"

"Yes, sir."

"Well. You might be in luck. One of my nurses failed to show up for work this morning. If he's out tomorrow too, perhaps you can have his place. Bring me proof of qualifications and your birth certificate tomorrow and I'll see if you're a good fit for the specialist care Mr Axton needs."

The camera blurs on Finch's back as he walks away and Tomas sits down. "Someone not show up? Does that happen often?"

Tomas's new best friend shrugs. "Never really thought about it. Be a shame if he got the sack for a hangover."

"What do you mean?"

"It was Ryan's twenty-first yesterday. I covered his shift for him. He probably got drunk and he lives on his own so his folks wouldn't wake him up, clattering about, like mine do."

There's a minute or two of chat during which they learn that Tom's new friend is an intern, nineteen years old, called Faizal Alam, plans to go to college after the summer to study healthcare management, and has just handed in his notice because he finds Axton creepy.

Faizal looms as he leans closer to Tomas. "You should hear the things the old man says. Maybe then you'd change your mind about working for him. Makes my skin crawl to hear him talk about his carers. He asks about all their families. Said I wasn't worth the effort of getting to know. I'm not taking that shit. Finch doesn't care. He gets paid well. I mean, have you seen his car?"

Paulina stops the presentation and looks around the table. "So. Do we think Axton has struck again? Is this missing nurse…" She flips through her notes. "Mr Ryan Eccles, still alive?"

Marion nods. "I think so. But he'll be weakening as Axton feeds off his strength."

"We ought to hand this over to the police," Alex says.

Several pairs of eyes tell him he's an idiot. Oonagh sighs. "You want to go to them with the whole story? You'll be laughed out of the station at best, or banged up for wasting police time."

"But the missing person—"

"Isn't officially missing. I checked. No Misper report. No family. They'll tell you he's a fit and healthy young man, to try tracking his phone and calling the hospitals then wait and see if he shows up in a few days."

Alex shakes his head. "So we do nothing? We let this man die to feed that…that thing?"

"No." Heads turn as Sarah speaks out. "We find him, whatever state he's in. We bring him back and end Axton. We just need to get to him." She looks at Alex. "With Harry, if what I have heard is correct."

"Griffin," Alex says. "Is that possible? I mean, I have only ever communicated with him in my house, mostly in the main bedroom. Isn't he stuck there?"

"He could move if he needed to." Marion aims a covert wink at Alex. "He needs a little help."

Marion and Sarah watch Alex intently. "What?" he says, warily. Jaspreet is gaping at him.

"You could take him," Marion replies, face a careful study of innocence. "You have an unusually strong connection."

Alex frowns. "What do you mean? Is he buried under my house or something? Do I need to—"

"No," Sarah shakes her head. "I expect if he'd been down there the excavators would have found his remains when your house was built. Marion means you can carry him as part of you. If you will allow it, and if he is willing."

"You're actually saying," Jaspreet blurts out, "you actually found an actual ghost?"

Alex's frown deepens. "All right. Let's say, for the sake of argument, that I have absolutely no idea what you're all talking about."

Paulina plays the rest of Tomas's video and Oonagh summarizes his increasingly persuasive conversations with Faizal, who is more than happy to 'stick it to the boss.' Then Marion and Sarah take Alex through their plan step-by-step. Tomas will let them into the mansion. Once inside, as a final fuck-you to his creepy employer, Faizal has agreed to get them inside Axton's private suite. Harry – no, Griffin in Alex's body – will distract Axton while Faizal and Tomas find Ryan Eccles. Sarah will perform an exorcism ceremony to sever Axton's hold on Ryan. Marion will coordinate everyone's actions while Jaspreet stays on his phone and keeps a look out. Paulina and Oonagh will record everything.

"Easy," Alex says in a flat voice, sitting back with a deep sigh. "What could possibly go wrong."

"Well," Sarah admits quietly, "many things. But Harry will be able to say goodbye. He'll find peace, if he wants it." Alex finds Sarah and Marion watching him again. "You can say goodbye too."

Alex pushes his chair back and leaves the room. Jaspreet catches up with him in the foyer. "Alex? Wait. What's going on? Tell me–"

"No!" Alex stops. Jaspreet faces him. Marion is close behind. "It's too much," Alex says, looking from Jaspreet's concerned expression to Marion's resolute, grim face. "What if Tomas's friend changes his mind? What if we can't get to Axton? What if he's too strong?"

"What if we fail," Marion says with exasperation. "What if we don't? What if, what if, what if. Would you like to go home and tell him there's a chance to give him peace, only you're so frightened you're giving up before the first step?" Alex takes a deep breath, closes his eyes and clenches his fists. He wants nothing more than to go home, take his meds and dream of Griffin. "Go home," Marion says as if she can read his mind. "Ask him what he wants."

"Okay," Alex says, letting out his breath in a long hiss. "Okay."

"Good. I'll tell them we're meeting at your house tonight."

Refusing Jaspreet's offer to drive him, Alex goes home in a daze and takes his anxiety meds as soon as he is inside. He lies on his bed and waits. "Griffin," he says when he feels the air chill. "I need to see you."

No.

The voice is in his head rather than in his ear. He feels cold fingertips trail across his lips and tries to kiss them as they pass. "Do you know what Marion plans?"

Yes.

Cold lips on his cheek. Alex turns his head but misses them. "Can I carry you? How does that even work? Will I be…myself?"

I'm already here, love, Griffin's voice says in his head. *We both are. Get some sleep. We both need your strength.*

Alex wakes up in darkness to the sound of his doorbell.

He feels faintly silly but a little excited as they walk up to the staff entry gate and through without so much as a squeak thanks to Tomas' security card. Nobody pays them any attention as Sarah, in headscarf and cassock and dog-collar, walks ahead arm in arm with Marion, who is doing her best to look like a confused resident. Alex, Paulina and Oonagh go with Tomas to get into the red scrubs Faizal has stashed in the staff changing room for them, while Faizal introduces himself to Marion in his loudest, most condescending voice, promising to help her find her room. Jaspreet waits outside, phone in his hand, hopping from foot to foot, and watches the gate and the door.

Alex is calm as he slips on red scrubs and soft shoes. For Griffin's sake, he has to be.

Marion and Oonagh go with Tomas to the rooms where, by a process of elimination based on furtively trying door handles earlier in his shift, Faizal has decided the missing carer must be. Alex, Sarah, and Paulina follow Faizal to Axton's private suite. "Brace yourselves," Faizal says quietly. "He's not what you might expect."

"I know." Alex hears himself speak but the words are a surprise to him. "I've seen him." Alex turns to look down on Sarah's careworn face. "I'm sorry about Uncle Matthew," he...no. Griffin says, with his voice, only his accent is strange. "I couldn't reach him to tell him it wasn't his fault."

Sarah smiles. "I know, Harry."

There's a cool hand on his cheek and a hot prickle of tears. "Come on," Griffin says. "Let's end this."

Alex stares through eyes that feel like they are not entirely his. There's a man, tall and gaunt with the hollow cheeks of someone who has not seen enough food for months. He has translucent, papery skin spider-webbed with red capillaries, and he is staring out from under a few wisps of greasy yellow hair with grayish, watery eyes that remind Alex of the milky bullseyes he used to play with in the schoolyard. For a moment, he thinks they are too late and Axton is already dead from extreme old age. "Don't be fooled," a wary, nervous voice in his head tells him.

The skeletal figure sits up and raises an arm to point at Alex. "I see you brought back the one that got away," Axton says in a thin, papery whisper that sets Alex's teeth on edge. "So kind. I can finish my feast. Harry, come closer! Let Mr Axton see you again, my boy."

Alex feels his bones freeze. He's dimly aware of Sarah chanting in the background, voice firm. Griffin's terror suffuses his whole being and it is all he can do not to turn tail and bolt from the room, but Sarah's chanting anchors him. Axton laughs, a thin, sibilant wheeze that wets his lip and chin. "Running won't do you any good, boy. I can see you now and I will find you again. Now. Come closer. Give me what's mine."

Alex's feet move despite his resistance. Faizal surges forward, blocking the path to Axton's bedside, and with a gesture of Axton's arm, is thrown aside as if he were a doll. Alex's head spins. He's gasping for breath and his ears are buzzing and ringing louder and louder.

"No!"

The word is barely a breath. Nearby, Sarah chants over and over and over. He mouths Sarah's words, recognizing and understanding the Latin from Harry's memories of Matthew's books, anticipating the ritual as she speaks. As his feet reluctantly drag him within Axton's reach, he's blinded by a bolt like blue-white lightning. His world buzzes and dims into nothing.

He wakes up in an unfamiliar bed with faces he thinks he should recognize regarding him with concern. "Take it easy," an elderly woman says. "You've had a rough time."

He blinks although the lights are dimmed. "Marion?"

There's a laugh. Another pair of eyes peer into his. "I'm right here, too."

Panic descends and he tries to get up. "Axton—"

"No, no, relax," Marion pushes gently on his shoulder. "We were in time. There's nothing left of the creature but dust. The boy, Ryan, he's going to be okay. Axton hadn't touched him yet."

He sighs deeply and lies back, blinking away tears. There's someone he's forgotten. Someone who should be here with him. He struggles to sit up although the effort makes his vision go gray. "Where's my Alex?"

Marion laughs kindly and the other woman joins in. He has a flash of understanding, or perhaps a memory suddenly clicks, a vision of those intensely appraising eyes in a different face. No, not different, not really. Just younger. "Sarah? Little Sarah?"

The hard, appraising eyes soften and blink away tears. "Yes! It's me, Harry. You've been lost for so long I began to think Matthew was wrong and we'd never find you again."

"Where is he. Where's Alex?" Harry tries to sit up again. "I want Alex. Where is he?"

"I'm here, Griffin." Harry looks at the doorway. Alex is there, supported by Faizal on one side and a crutch on the other. "I felt you wake up. I had to see if you were real. Really real."

"Well now," Marion says, smirking at Harry. "I suppose visiting time is over. We'll be just outside the door."

Faizal steers Alex over to the chair nearest Harry's bedside, sees him settled then retreats after Sarah and Marion. Alex looks at Harry and smiles. Harry watches him warily. "Hello, Alex."

"Hello, Griffin."

"What the fuck happened."

Alex can't suppress the feeling that bubbles up and bursts out of his throat as a half-strangled sob. "I thought you might tell me. Marion told me the exorcism was successful. Axton hadn't had time to take your life entirely." Alex hiccups and his voice cracks. "And when Axton was…I don't know, sent back? He couldn't take you with him. He had to give it all up. Everything he had taken from you."

Alex is quiet for a minute. "Everything," he repeats. "Your body was still in that basement room, walled off, but you showed me where it was. Jas and Faizal broke through. And there you were. Unconscious, barely alive, but there. Real."

Alex sobs again and covers his face with his hands until he recovers. "The floor was burned where the markings had been. Reverend Sarah exorcized the entire place just in case." He takes a deep breath and looks at Harry with reddened eyes. "Marion said you fought him off. All those years ago. And you chose to stay to see him destroyed." Alex clutches at Harry's hand. "You are real, aren't you? Am I hallucinating? Dreaming you up?"

Gasping with the effort, Harry struggles up onto his elbows and beckons Alex closer. Their lips meet in a desperate kiss. As Harry collapses back onto his pillows and Alex crashes back onto the chair, Alex asks again. "Are you really, *really* here?"

Harry grins and bangs his knuckles on the side table once.

It's late summer and the garden is in full and glorious bloom thanks to the attention it has had this year. Alex reads over the new lease again. "So, the owners will raise the rent next year but have kept it in line with the consumer price index this year."

"Yes," Claire says, pointing to the clause that details future rent increases. "That's standard. Actually they want to get the place on the market now that you got rid of the, um, ghost problem."

"Ghost problem?"

Harry puts three glasses of lemonade on the little patio table.

He throws himself into an aluminum chair, which squeaks its protest. "Since when were ghosts a problem?"

Claire sucks her lip and frowns. "Do you need to be added to the lease? You'll need proof of current address, bank details, and an employer reference."

"No," Alex says with a smile and a shake of his head. "It's just me for now. Where do I sign?"

Claire's face clears. "Initial every page, then we both sign and date where I put the stickers."

With a grin that he will have to explain later, Alex turns to Harry and says, "Sweetheart, do you have a pen?"

WISHES

"Robbie?"

Ma's cheery voice sailed over the top of the calls and whistles of the stable boys and the snorts and whinnies of the Master's Suffolks, busy being freed from their harnesses and turned out to pasture, where they found a small reserve of energy for playfulness before settling down to the serious business of grazing. Robbie watched with wide-eyed delight as one of the huge work horses approached, bringing their slightly sweet, earthy-scented air with them, and accepted a palmful of grain with surprisingly gentle lips and a warm, ticklish puff from flaring nostrils. He, for Robbie had been sure of that since learning that girls and boys were different in every way that mattered to him and a few ways that didn't, giggled and reached into his pockets for more of the treats he'd stolen from the grain buckets earlier.

"Robbie!"

Ma's voice pushed through the stamping and huffing from the three other Suffolks who had come to see what they were missing out on. Robbie apologized profusely for only having two hands with which to feed them and two pockets in which to hide illicit treats, and stroked each long nose that came within reach. He turned and slid down off the post and rail fence when he heard Ma's voice almost right behind him.

"Robbie, there you are, sweetheart." She smiled, pale skin spattered with freckles and framed with russet hair. "Been looking after the horses again?"

He nodded. "I was allowed to help out again. I used the big rake to clean out the stalls while the lads polished the saddles. Henry watched me. I was fine."

"So that's why you stink, girl." Ma held out her hands. "Let's get you cleaned up before Gramma sees you." Ma wrinkled her nose and laughed. "Or smells you."

Robbie looked down at his stained boots. He'd done his best to tuck his skirts out of the way but there was nothing to be done about his feet. "Ma, can I look after the stables when I'm big enough? Mister Henry says I'm good with the horses. He let me ride Coira's new gelding and Coira thought it a lark."

"Did he now?" Ma said with a warning in her voice. "I might have words with that Henry. Man with daughters himself ought to know better and that Miss Coira is a law unto herself."

Robbie's sun-pink face flushed deeper and he patted Ma's arm then grabbed it and pulled her to a halt. "No, Ma. I don't want to get them in any bother. I asked a hundred times before Henry said yes. He's good to me."

"Well," Ma sighed and found another smile. "I suppose there's no harm in it. Just be careful, princess. Don't want you falling off and banging that pretty head of yours or getting upset when you're told off for forgetting to say *Miss* Coira and curtseying up at the house."

Robbie smiled up at Ma and swept a few wavy copper strands back from his white face, reminding himself with a sharp intake of breath that the side of his forehead still ached from his stumble the day before, tripping and falling and hitting his head after ducking the empty threat of a backhander from Da. It had felt real at the time and Da's call of "clumsy lass" had made it ache all the more. Ma's face set like stone and she leaned over to plant a soft kiss beside the purple and blue.

"Come on," Ma said, bright and brittle. "Let's go sit by the well for a minute. I know you'll've had some coins off the lads for your hard work. Maybe you can spend a little one on wishes."

Robbie took Ma's hand and let himself be led away from the stables, away from the paddocks, away from his huge, equine friends, and sat on the lip of the well. Ma drew a pail of water and set about cleaning Robbie's boots while he jingled the few small coins in his pocket, pulled out a palmful, sorted them by size and luster, and put the best ones back. He looked up at the lined, smiling face of his mother and dropped a copper halfpenny into the well, cupping his hand behind his ear to listen out for the tiniest splash.

"Make a wish!"

He shrugged. "What should I wish for, Ma?"

"Anything that'll make you happy, my sweet! But never tell a soul until after it comes true. If you tell, it spoils the spell." Ma smoothed a tangle from Robbie's long hair, mindful of the goose-egg. She leaned over and kissed the crown of his head. "Not even your old ma. Go on, Robbie, give 'er another. You'll not buy your heart's desire with a halfpenny."

Robbie jingled his pocket again. He chose a penny dulled brown with tarnish, twice as big as the last coin, as if that would make his fervent wishes twice as likely to come true. He closed his eyes and smiled when he heard the faint splash.

"Shall I have one more try for us both?" Ma raised her eyebrows and held out her hand, palm up. Robbie nodded and held his fist over his ma's flat palm and let all the rest of his treasure fall into it. Ma shifted and sorted the coins in her hand, chose the biggest, shiniest silver one, and held it out over the well where Robbie could see it glint in the sunlight.

"Shut your eyes, make your wishes, and hold my hand," she

instructed, and Robbie obeyed. He closed his eyes and wished and wished and wished, imagining how the shiny silver coin – the lucky one with the funny picture on it that he'd found between the cobblestones in town and polished every week at Gramma's scullery table – would tumble and fall like a speck of glitter into the darkness. He listened and listened and listened for a splash that never came.

"Oh well," said Ma, deftly pocketing the silver coin she hadn't dropped because the rent was due and Da had worked only four days and not the whole week, then she took Robbie's other hand too.

"Sometimes we have to make our wishes come true all by ourselves." Ma laughed and Robbie smiled at the light in her pale, freckled face. "Right now, I wish I had a warm kitchen and some apple fritters with honey. You're going to help me make my wishes come true."

Later, when he reached for Gramma's polish in the scullery, he'd miss that special coin and bite back tears for its loss while Gramma held court with her severe iron hair pinned back from her rosy face and dealt out advice to all who'd listen (and all who'd not) as she made the silver gleam for the Master and Mistress. And that night, as he lay pretending to sleep on his bed, unrolled under the kitchen table of the two-room cottage he shared with Ma and Da, he heard murmurs from Ma then Da sobbing softly and promising one more time that he'd never lose a day's work on account of the demon drink again. Still, Robbie thought with a pang of guilt and his bottom lip held fast between his teeth, his first wish was for it to be just him and Ma, and he hadn't changed his mind about that.

He had almost forgotten the walk by the well when his first wish came true. It was so many months later that the bottoms of his skirts and the tops of the boots that pinched his toes didn't overlap any more. Despite him having let down the hem as far as he could, the spring breeze nipped at his shins when he went out at dawn to cluck at the chickens and throw them some grain. Da was already on his way out and Robbie wondered later if he would have said goodbye if he'd known what was to occur that afternoon.

He heard it from John the ploughman, up at the barn after Da was carried inside and covered up. Robbie stood pale-faced and wide-eyed with his hands gripping the back of Ma's pinafore until his knuckles went white and his arms ached.

"He just dropped," John said with a pitiful shrug and a quiet voice that seemed to diminish the big man's stature. His thick brown fingers with cracked, pale fingernails picked at a frayed patch in the woven cap in his hands. "We went out with the new Clydesdales, getting them accustomed to the harnesses and the pull of the plough, ready to break soil for the spring sowing, when he just stopped." John took a deep breath. "He fell where he stood, Bridie. There weren't anything I could do for him, my girl. I told them he worked the whole day. I waited and finished the job and told them up there," John hiked a thumb towards the House where (like all the farm workers) he was not allowed to venture, "that it happened at the end of the day. I brought him back on Samson while I walked Delilah. So you'll get what he's due for the full day and the Master'll pay for the…for the arrangements."

Ma stood in stony silence then reached behind her to grasp and squeeze Robbie's tight fists. He released his grip, shook out his aching hands and slid his arm through Ma's in case she needed the support. But Ma stood upright, strong as ever, so Robbie inched closer to the sack-covered lump that used to be called Da.

"Thank you for your kindness," Ma said quietly to John, then noticed Robbie reaching for the corner of the sack. "Robbie, no. Don't look. It's not him any more."

"Why not let her see?" John said quietly. "Same happens to all of us when it's our time."

Ma reached her hand out to Robbie and he took it. "I won't if you say no," he said quietly. "I just."

"I know," Ma said. "He was–"

"Your Georgie was a good man," John said, slapping his hat back on his head. "I'm sorry for your loss."

"Yes," Ma said.

"Yes," echoed Robbie, because it seemed like the right thing to say.

Three days later Robbie stood in stern silence under a warm spring sun because he'd been told it was rude to smile by the graveside. When the prayers were over and the small knot of bare-headed men and veil-covered women began to disperse, Robbie walked up to the gravedigger who stood like a sentry a little way off.

"Give me that," Robbie said, pointing at the shovel in the man's gnarled hand and pulling off his own bonnet and veil.

"Your ma'll give me hell if I let her little princess dirty her apron," he replied with a wink and a smile that Robbie did not like in the slightest. "This isn't a job for a girl."

"I'll see him buried," Robbie insisted, reaching for the shovel, clasping it firmly and pulling against his resistance. "He was my Da. I owe him that. I've the right since I've got no brothers to bury him for me."

"The right?" The gravedigger scoffed. "I suppose you think you do."

He let go suddenly and Robbie sprawled backwards to the sound of laughter. Red faced and gritting his teeth with anger but saving it for good use, he pushed to his feet, turned and marched to the pile of earth beside the newest hole in the ground, thrusting the shovel in deep. The shovel sank in easily at first and he levered up as much of the rich brown earth as he could carry, tipping it off into the grave and listening to the thump and rattle as soil and stones hit thin wood. Since it was just him and Da now, he allowed himself a grim smile and went back for more. Shovel after shovel of earth slipped into the grave until soil only landed on more soil. But despite the strength he'd earned working in the stables whenever he had the chance, the longer he worked the harder it became to lift the shovel. By the time he had moved enough earth to cover the coffin completely, his arms and back ached and his hands burned and stung with new blisters beside old calluses.

"Give it up, sweet," the gravedigger called from his seat under a chestnut tree. "It's no job for a little lass."

"I'm not a little lass!" Robbie shouted. He hurled one more shovel, as full as he could bear, into the grave and screamed after it, yelling words he had only heard from Da in the worst of his tempers.

"Now that's enough," the gravedigger snapped, wrenching the shovel from Robbie's hands. "Show respect for your poor old Da. Grief'll only excuse so much. You get back to your Ma and leave this job to the men."

Robbie grabbed his discarded and trampled bonnet and veil, and ran. When he clung to Ma and burst into furious tears, unable to articulate why he wept, he supposed it must be that he missed Da since that was what everyone who saw him said.

The day after the funeral it felt to Robbie like Da had barely existed. He helped Ma pack away Da's things from the room and kitchen of the tiny cottage. When they had cleared his presence from their home, a labor of perhaps half an hour, only a bundle of the Sunday Best Ma refused to see buried with him and a box containing a chipped stoneware tankard, a pipe, a knife and a shaving kit remained as evidence that he'd ever lived there.

"I'll take his good clothes to market next time I get to go into town," Ma said with a nod. "We'll get something for them. I'll take his other bits to the House and maybe some of the men can have them as remindings." Ma flashed Robbie a frown. "Unless you want to keep something?"

Robbie pressed his lips tight and shook his head.

For the next two weeks, Robbie would wake before the sun, ease himself from the warmth of the fold out bed he now shared with Ma, wash and dress at the basin in the little kitchen with a sliver of soap pilfered from the kitchen at the House and water from the rain barrels Da had set up to fill from the gutters. He would wake Ma and she'd perform the same ablutions while Robbie tidied their room. On some days, when fewer hands were called for up at the house, Ma would send Robbie to the schoolhouse where he'd spend the morning helping the little ones practice their letters and numbers for an hour or two to earn the reward of being allowed time for reverent study of the pages of the schoolmaster's modest but prized collection of books. His favorite had pages crammed with the outlines and names of far distant places, and descriptions of lands that sounded utterly fantastical.

Perhaps when he was older and more learned, and Master Arnold was no more (already not a young man by Robbie's standards), Robbie wondered if he might travel and study too, then take over the school, dressed in breeches and a woolen jacket, and live in the attic room above the heads of the scribbling children. When Robbie mentioned his aspirations one day after the youngsters ran for home at the end of lessons, Master Arnold thought the idea so ridiculous that his normally sallow cheeks turned red as he roared with derision. This was partly because he was, in fact, only thirty-seven and partly because, as he explained with a quiet scoff, "Maybe if you start in service soon and work your way up, make yourself agreeable, you might be a nursery maid after the young Miss Coira marries. But someone lacking a genteel upbringing is in no position to hope for higher than that."

That was the last day Robbie bothered to attend school. Instead, he'd wish Ma a good day and double back after her. But rather than following Ma to the back of the House and presenting himself at the kitchens for the chance of a day's casual labor in the scullery or the laundry, he skirted around to the paddocks and the stables where he could make himself useful by tying his long red plait up tight, hitching up his skirts and pinafore then helping to muck out the stalls, polish the brasses and saddles, and stitch repairs in the strong but pliant leather.

One of the lads, a pale, quietly sullen boy called Lucas, took a shine to Robbie and often chose to work beside him, stealing glances at Robbie's coppery hair and green eyes. Robbie pretended not to notice but the attention was flattering, nonetheless.

"You ever seen where we all live?" Lucas asked abruptly one

afternoon, leaning across the smooth seat of the master's very best saddle set on a bale between them. They crouched one on either side of the expanse of tawny leather with polishing rags while the bigger lads waited with blankets, looking out for the master's hunting party to return with sweating, thirsty beasts.

"No," Robbie replied, jerking his head upwards to the loft above the animal stalls. "Up there?"

Lucas nodded and grinned, pink splotches appearing on his neck and cheeks. "Come and see."

Curiosity won over Robbie's fear of what Ma would say about it if she knew. He stood up, draped the polishing rag over the pommel and followed Lucas up the narrow ladder to the loft, its gloom lifted by sunlight from a square window, unglazed but with shutters that could be closed to keep the wind and rain out. Robbie looked around, surprised by how orderly it was with spaces divided up with bales of hay and straw. Lucas linked one arm with Robbie's and pointed with the other. "That's Tobias. That's Colm. That's Archie. And this is me."

At the word *me*, Lucas cupped his free hand firmly on one of the slight swells of Robbie's chest, pulled him closer by his trapped arm, and kissed him sloppily on the lips. Robbie recoiled, shook his head and cursed, shoved Lucas off with the extra strength granted by his flash of anger and shame at having been tricked, then retreated, red-faced, back down to the stables below. He shut out the raucous whooping and the rousing round of applause from the other boys, marched right out of the stable doors into the cobbled yard where earlier the horses' hooves had clattered as they got ready for their day's exercise, and stood with his arms wrapped tightly around his chest and his teeth set in a snarl of rage.

"Robbie!" Lucas called out from the open door. "It were a joke. Don't take it bad. Come back and help me finish up the polishing. Mister Henry won't pay you if you're not here to be paid."

Closing his eyes and taking a deep breath, squeezing his arms to himself tighter and tighter, Robbie felt the anger change. It didn't evaporate like puddles in the wind or seep away like rain on a thirsty field, but it felt like he'd compressed it so firmly that he'd packed it solid into a new feeling. Determination that he wasn't to be the butt of jokes. Determination that he was more than what those boys saw of him. Determination that he would, somehow, show them all. Slowly, Robbie relaxed his expression, dropped his arms, turned around and walked back to the stables. On his way past Lucas's grinning face, he back-fisted the boy sharply between the legs. Lucas gasped, groaned, and doubled over.

"It were a joke," Robbie said loudly as the older boys hooted with laughter, this time at their friend's expense. "Don't take it bad."

Lucas and the other boys didn't bother Robbie after that. Tobias and Colm moved on to other jobs with better wages, Lucas spoke back to Mister Henry twice and was dismissed, and Archie took over the care of the new stable lads. Robbie kept to himself, choosing the outdoor work where he could, so that he could keep his distance. June days stretched out long into July. The Master and Mistress entertained more, so more help was needed as the paddocks and stable blocks filled up with horses belonging to guests. Robbie always found the time to nip in and out of the stores to pocket handfuls of grain and carrots deemed too tough to serve at table, and feed them to whichever of his favorites came nickering and snorting over the fence of the near paddock.

On a sweltering, still day in the middle of the month when Robbie fetched two pails of water from the well to top up one of the troughs, the fussy old dapple-gray gelding that had once had the honor of being the young Miss Coira's first proper mount, ambled over to snort in Robbie's face and try to bite at his pockets for the goodies he always carried. Robbie laughed, stepped back and offered a few pieces of rubbery carrot. "There you go, Silver, you old git," he said, scratching Silver's head behind the ear. "Wish Ma and Gramma had an old age as easy as yours to look forward to."

Towards the end of summer, when children too young for work

anticipated lessons on reading and writing and counting in the musty schoolroom down in the village, Ma took Robbie's hand in the fading warmth of the gloaming as they went inside their tiny cottage and gave it a gentle squeeze. She smiled a little sadly. "Da's not here to bring home the bacon any more and rent's due again already," she said, and Robbie felt another squeeze of his fingers. "I know you had your heart set on being a genteel school mistress, but–"

"Ma," Robbie replied, "I thought I'd–"

"You'll hear me out, Robbie," Ma said sharply, and Robbie saved his words for when Ma was ready to listen to them. "I'm sorry for it," Ma continued in a level, matter-of-fact voice that showed she'd rehearsed. "But we can't afford for you not to be earning in proper, regular work instead of day-work. I'll take you up to the House tomorrow instead of sending you to lessons and we'll get you started. Alice the scullery maid got caught with that stable lad, Archie, and both've been dismissed. So, there's an opening if you get in quick. If the both of us work up at the House, we'll get digs too. There's Alice's space in the attic. It's small but it's big enough for us." Ma paused and took a deep breath, and Robbie waited for the deciding fact. "Henry says there's a family man starting who needs the cottage more."

Robbie's heart swelled and beat so hard he could hear the blood rushing in his ears and his stomach fluttered. "Ma, I could be the stable lad," he said, words tumbling and splashing like a spill on the red tiled pantry floor. "I could! I seen them work and I helped out loads when you were busy on Gramma's orders."

Ma laughed and hugged Robbie as if he'd told a joke. "Oh, princess, they'll not let you do that. Not for real. Care for the horses in skirts and clean linen pinafore?"

"Then I won't wear skirts and a pinnie." Bright eyed, Robbie smiled as a nebulous plan coalesced in his head. Ma couldn't be told, he knew that from experience, but he'd make sure she would see him for who he was. "I'll show you, I will. Tomorrow."

"Of course you will." Ma shook her head. "Now let me do your hair neat for bed. We'll get to sleep early and first thing I'll take you up to Gramma and get you in."

Set on a plan, Robbie waited until Ma's breaths came out even and slow then slipped out of bed and opened the curtain to let the bright, silver moon light up his work. With sharp shears and strong, nimble fingers accustomed to work, eyes used to the dark and ears attuned to the slightest sign of Ma's waking, the transformation began. Da's old shirt – the good one that Ma promised to sell or trade but somehow always forgot to take to market with her – got its sleeves shortened and its width narrowed with clever tucks and darts. The brown woolen Sunday breeches got turn-ups so Robbie could let them down if he stretched even taller, then got trimmed and taken in enough at the seams that he could claim "room to grow" and hold them up using Da's old belt with extra holes punched through the leather with an awl.

Almost forgotten, last of all as the full disk of the moon slipped low in the sky leaving Robbie in pre-dawn darkness, a long red-gold plait tumbled to the floor. Robbie ran his hands through his inexpertly shorn hair, marveling at the sense of lightness and freedom, and wondering for the first time if he was a fool to think Ma wouldn't be angry or ashamed of him once her surprise wore off, wondering if Ma would understand that she'd always had a son to be proud of. But in the same predawn darkness, Robbie felt something new as he shucked off his nightdress and put on his new clothes. A comforting yet enticing sense of rightness settled in his ribcage and calmed his fears about the hours to come. He adjusted his shirt, glad that there was little to hide yet about his work-strong shape, and lay down to doze for as long as he was allowed.

"Get up, Robbie!" Ma's voice startled Robbie into reluctant wakefulness. "Up! If I'm late I get an earful from Gramma. Let's get you up to the House bright and early so you get a full day in too."

Robbie emerged from the blanket, yawned and stretched in gray dawn light, then rubbed at an unexpected draught across his bare neck. Ma stared, mouth flapping soundlessly for the few seconds it took to gather her wits.

"What in the name of – what have you done to yourself, my girl!"

"I'm not your girl, Ma." Robbie stood up and brushed creases from his breeches, tucked his shirt in again and fastened his belt. "I won't be a maid and curtsey and scurry around guarding what's under my skirts. I'll be a stable boy and stand up tall and tend to the horses."

Ma took a step back and frowned, looking Robbie up and down. Robbie waited, chewing at his lip, feet rooted to the spot, fear of what Ma might say and do worrying at his nerves. His head felt like it was stuck staring forwards and down, unable to turn to follow Ma's progress as she walked all around him.

"You can't just–"

Ma bit off her words, sucked her lips, frowned and tutted, looked Robbie up and down a few more times, then shook her head and sighed. "I suppose at least we won't be needing to make you a new dress this winter and your Da's old clothes are getting some use. Well, I couldn't part with them so why shouldn't you have them." Ma ran her hand through Robbie's hair, what was left of it, shook her head and tutted again. "No. That won't do at all. You better bring me the shears and the stool. Looks like you cut all your lovely hair off with a scythe."

Robbie fetched the shears from the table he'd worked at most of the night and handed them to Ma. Ma pointed at the stool he'd sat on, and he sat there again, moving his head this way and that under the guidance of Ma's silent pushes and shoves. Only the regular snipping of the shears disturbed the air in the little room, and copper hairs cascaded down his shoulders to curl on the floor. He remembered Da sitting here too on the first Sunday of every month, growling about this or that while Ma took his hair back to an inch. Robbie wondered if he'd look like Da when the job was done.

A few minutes later, Ma rubbed her hands over Robbie's head

to dislodge loose strands that glinted as they caught the morning light. She hummed and nodded. "Might get away with it," she said, "if you can keep it up. Stable boys get better pay than scullery maids, I suppose, and I don't believe the work is any harder."

Sudden doubt frayed at Robbie's resolve. "Ma, what if they recognize me up at the house?"

"They'll not see little Roberta in her skirts and pinafore when they look at you unless you let it slip yourself." Ma said sharply. "So if this is what your heart is set on, you make sure to keep your nerve and see it through." Robbie blinked away the prickle behind his eyelids. Ma laughed. "Tell you something, though." She reached for the top of Robbie's head and ruffled the short hair that twisted itself into curls now that it was not weighted by length, and pulled him into a tight hug. "You make a handsome little prince."

Robbie could have run to the stables, but Ma held his hand until they were in sight of the House. Henry was in the yard with Silver, walking the gelding in circles.

"Heard there's an opening for a stable boy, Mister Henry," Robbie said, then he coughed and took Silver's harness from the older man. Silver snorted and nosed at Robbie's hip, looking for pockets. He lowered the pitch of his voice. "On account of a lad having been dismissed."

Henry blinked deep brown eyes set in sockets ringed with dark shadows and frowned at Robbie. "News travels fast, lad," he said. "Are you used to hard work?"

Robbie pulled himself up as tall as possible and looked Henry in the eye. "I got experience," he said, resuming the perimeters Henry had been plodding with Silver and increasing the pace to a brisk walk for the pony. "I done mucking out, feeding, saddling, polishing, mending, checking if the blacksmith's needed, caring for the likes of this old fellow with the bellyache and–"

Henry held up a hand and laughed. "All right," he said, shaking his cloud of white hair. "Silver likes you and that's as good a reference as you'll get around here. You take good care of him and I'll give you a trial to the end of the week. What's your name, lad?"

"Rob–" Robbie started to say then cut off his own name.

"I'll need more than that to write in the books, lad."

Robbie thought about his Da and his Ma, weighed and measured Georgie Plowman against Bridie Kerry, and chose the one he liked the sound of more. "Kerry. I'm Rob Kerry."

"Well, Rob Kerry," Henry said, calling back over his shoulder as he walked away towards his own digs. "There's a space in the hayloft for you." He stopped and looked back, sucking his teeth, at Robbie who was still making Silver walk off the colic. "If you think that's the best place for you to sleep."

Robbie frowned but Henry apparently didn't notice. "Silver my old man," Robbie said to the gelding, "I owe you all the carrots you want when you're feeling better."

Silver stopped and pulled hard on Robbie's grip, rolled onto his back a couple of times and let out a loud eruption of gas that lasted several seconds. Robbie covered his mouth and laughed. "You evil old donkey," he said, pulling on Silver's bridle. "Come on. I know you can do worse than that."

By late morning, Rob had Silver stabled and comfortable, and he stood in Silver's stall brushing him then combing and braiding his mane, all the while telling him what a good and clever pony he was. The other stable lads barely gave him a second glance as they went about their tasks, glad that they were out of reach of old Silver's nipping teeth and stamping hooves. At dinner time, Rob sat on a straw bale with the other lads and slurped his share of stew from the pot he'd been sent to collect from Gramma up at the House. And after he'd rinsed out the dishes and walked back up to the kitchen door with them, at bedtime he climbed into the hayloft and claimed the vacant space for himself. There was a bundle waiting for him, tied tight with twine and labelled with his new name written in Ma's block capitals. He cut the twine with his pocket-knife and shook it open to find his old bedroll from the cottage, a worn but serviceable undershirt, a pair of long-johns and, to his horror, a lady's bodice that he guessed from the size and the mending must have been cast off by Miss Coira.

As he folded the clothing in the fading twilight from the square window in the gable end beside his allocated space and set out his blankets on fresh straw that would poke and itch all night, Rob noticed that another item had fallen out. He picked it up and inspected the carefully tied bundle of fabric pads and Ma's handwriting – *you will be wanting these regardless and you could make the corset fit a boy* – on a scrap of paper torn from a household accounts book. Rob's face blossomed pink when he recognized what they were for. Ma had explained to him as soon as he was twelve what 'the blessing' was but he'd pushed it far, far from his mind. He sat down and bundled the pads, tied around with their fabric belt, then stuffed them between the folds of his blankets. He would deal with that problem when it arose. The bodice he examined with a thoughtful frown that transformed into a wide smile when he realized why his Ma had sent it. If he strengthened the eyelets and altered the lacing and the shoulders just a little, he could wear it higher to flatten his shape, snug under his shirt.

Summer aged and nodded sleepily into autumn, and soon winter nipped sharply at autumn's toes as they kicked over drifts of copper and gold, then spring pushed snowdrops and crocuses through the dark earth while promising sparkling frosts before summer warmth returned. All through that year and the next, younger stable boys came and older ones went to take up positions that would earn them better wages or provide them with more comfortable beds. But Rob remained, so inevitably one day he was the oldest and had been there the longest. Henry clapped him on the shoulder after mucking out, a day after the previous head stable boy had gone to learn blacksmithing, and pointed out a younger boy trotting across the yard. "You'll be head stableman now, Kerry. Look after the new boy. See that you keep your stables in good order and don't be afraid to knock your lads into line."

"Yes sir," Rob replied, a swell of pride in his ribcage. "I'll do that."

Rob was a patient teacher who led by example. He was always

the first to rise so that he could perform his morning rituals in the privacy granted him by beasts who didn't care that he looked different from the other lads under his shirt and breeches. He was always the one who sauntered up to the House to fetch the day's breakfast and dinner from the kitchen door so that he could receive a kiss from Ma along with a cocked eyebrow that silently asked *is there anything else you need.* Rob assigned duties as fairly as he could with the harder jobs going to himself and the bigger lads, and on mornings when they were left to exercise the Master's horses themselves he'd lead the smallest lad out for a riding lesson on the most placid pony while Silver followed with neither saddle nor invitation. And, true to his word to Mister Henry, he was not above dealing out harsh tasks where harsh words had not worked.

He'd almost forgotten his three wishes at the well until the new lad asked over the suppertime stew if any of the others ever wished for a different life. Rob kept quiet as the lads all wished for ridiculous things. A hundred, no, a thousand gold coins. The bottomless purse of Fortunatus. To handfast with Miss Coira and be the Master one day. He thought of the wishes he had made at the well with Ma. His Da had gone, wished away by his first wish, he supposed with a pang of guilt. Then when he'd earned his position as head stable boy his second wish had come true, too.

His third wish... Rob joined in with the laughter at some fanciful desire of one of the lads to dine on pastries at every meal, and thought of the schoolmaster's old atlas and all the places he knew he'd never see, and of the stories he'd heard from Gramma, tales of goblins and spirits and knights and maidens.

"I once wished," he said when the lads' mirth died down, "that I could–"

He choked off the next word when Ma's rhyme came to his ears in Ma's singsong voice. If you tell, it spoils the spell. "I once wished that I could learn to ride and work with horses," he lied instead. "And my Ma said sometimes you have to make your wishes come true all by yourself. So that's what I did."

One night towards the end of summer, when black clouds obscured the sun, rain battered the stable roof, wind howled and whistled through the gaps, and the cracks and rumbles of lightning and thunder made the horses snort and stamp, Rob sat with the younger lads around a straw-bale table with a candle lit in a storm-lamp more for the cheer than the soft yellow light. He'd sent another to brave the dash to the kitchen door to fetch their meal and all that could be heard from the lads was the click and scrape of spoons in bowls. The animals were safe, and the lads were ready to huddle in the loft for comfort and warmth as if it were winter already. Guests that were expected had not come, and as he listened to the lads' minor grumbles, Rob hoped the party had sheltered in town and put off their arrival until the next day. But his hope was in vain. Rob's head shot up from his supper and his spoon stilled in the air, a few drops of broth splashing back into his bowl, at the clatter of hooves in the yard and a rough yell even louder than the storm.

"Boy?"

He could have been mistaken, imagining the hooves through the rain hammering on the roof and conjuring up the call from the sound of water splashing and gurgling from the gutters into the rain barrels.

"Boy!"

He scooped the last of his meal into his mouth, clattered his spoon and bowl to the floor beside his usual place, then scrambled out the door of the empty stall the lads were using as their dining room. The other stable boys, silenced for the few seconds it took to recognize that Rob would see to it and they were not needed yet, resumed their supper and chatter and complained about the mud they'd likely have to clean from hair, hooves, and boots. Rob pulled his coat tight against the rain and went out into the deluge to find out what was wanted of him.

A group of men waited with huffing, snorting, shivering beasts. The man at the front, handed over the reins of a huge animal. "Care for these horses well, boy," he said. "Especially my Friesian. He's worth more than you and this whole stable put together."

"Yessir," Rob replied, taking the rain-slicked creature, black as night with a silver gleam in his eye, by the bridle. He turned and called for his lads to help. The other men, all wearing brass buttoned jackets the color of slate, led the rest of the horses in and began the task of caring for their mounts. Before long, nine creatures were out of the rain, unsaddled or relieved of their packs, rubbed down and draped with damp-wicking wool, rewarded with chunks of carrot and handfuls of grain and housed in airy stalls with clean bedding and mangers of hay. The cavalry, for that was what Rob assumed all uniformed men to be, left in the direction of the barn. The man who had called him from his supper watched from the shelter of the doorway while the stable boys worked methodically by lantern light, taking Robbie's instructions without argument and reporting to him to inspect their work when done.

"Looks like you know what you're about," the man said with a nod. "How old are you?"

"Eighteen, sir," Rob replied. "Nineteen soon."

"You look younger." The man walked closer. Robbie held his ground. "Been a stable hand long?"

"Seven or eight years, more or less," Robbie said, keeping eye contact as if the man might challenge his decision to count into his experience all the time he was a willing helper for many thanks and few coins. In the lamplight the stranger's hazel eyes shone with amber and his hair looked as thick and golden as the sun itself. Rob's attention was captured by the neatly trimmed, short beard that graced the stranger's strong jaw, glinting with white here and there, catching the lamplight, and it flashed in his mind that he would like to rub the back of his fingers along it from ear to chin and back again, just to know whether it was bristly or soft. He felt his face warm up despite the cold air from the open door and tried to push the stray thought down deep.

"Well," the stranger said crisply, not seeing Rob's red-cheeked discomfort, "I might want to call for your services again, boy, if that's agreeable. What's do you call yourself?"

"Rob... Robert Kerry, sir," Rob said, swallowing, afraid his voice might fail him.

The stranger repeated more softly, "Robert Kerry, hmm," then left.

Chores completed for the night, leaving the supper dishes for morning rather than sending one of the lads back through the rain to be soaked, then cursed at by the scullery maid who now had guests to clean up after, Rob sent the lads to bed up in the hayloft, did one final round of the animals, then followed up the ladder to his own corner. The lads were lightening the gloom by laughing and joking with each other, describing with crude words and gestures what they wanted to do and which of the house maids or fancy-uniformed footmen they wanted to have warming their straw-stuffed beds. As usual, Rob laughed and whooped along with the banter, without adding anything about his own desires because he'd never been quite sure what his desires were.

He had his own ideas about sex, but Rob always dismissed the acts the stable lads giggled and guffawed about as wishful thinking at best, often calling them out as they slipped into the realms of pure fantasy. When Ma had instructed him on the subject years ago, making oblique references to 'woman parts' and 'man parts' that made him frown until Gramma translated using words that were not to be spoken in company, he'd shrugged and decided sex was something he might want in a future he hadn't imagined for himself at all. When he was ready. Whatever that meant.

That night, Rob's slow drift into slumber in the hayloft was made all the sweeter by imaginary soft glances and lingering touches from a tall, stern, blond-haired, hazel-eyed stranger who called his name gently and kissed him on the mouth. Under the drumming rain, the hayloft was full of the usual sounds: the soft noises of the animals below, the snorts and snores of some of the lads, and the quiet gasp and whimper from the two who always shared their warmth with each other, even in summer. *I might call for your services again*, he had said. Rob smiled, fingers pressed across his lips, and let his imagination run free on what might happen if the visiting lord came back for him.

The peculiar feeling low in his groin, not quite heat, not quite an itch, made Rob feel excited and warm and in want of something he couldn't quite name. He lay on his back and stretched out his legs, parted enough to slip his hand down his underclothes, and felt slick warmth there. It felt right, somehow, like he was fulfilling a desire for something he didn't even know he'd been missing. Rob stroked in the dampness, shivered and bit his lip as a whimper of his own threatened to surface. He imagined an act one of the lads had boasted about doing and let his fingers be guided by the growing feeling of rightness and his own fantasy. A fantasy of the way the lord's softly prickled cheek might feel against his thigh, of the way a tongue might feel in place of his fingers. Unable to stop if he'd even wanted to, legs spread wider, heels pushed hard into the edges of his straw-filled mattress, he rubbed faster until he tensed and gasped aloud, shaken by the intensity of the waves of pleasure he felt while the other stable boys nearby dreamed of maids and footmen and each other.

Rob woke early, as he always did, and scrambled down from the hayloft to be first to wash and dress in the darkness of Silver's stable. Around him, soft stamps and huffs welcomed him and he promised hay and grain and exercise soon, soon, soon, to every long nose that he patted and scratched on the way past to draw half a bucketful from the rain barrels, full to spilling from the overnight deluge. He rinsed himself clean and dried himself before pulling his cleanest underclothes back on and tightening the bodice that he had loosened for sleep. Once satisfied that his modesty was taken care of, he dressed properly, scrubbed his soiled underthings and hung them to dry.

Boots and voices came from the haylofts above as Rob hand-fed his favorite as a reward for sharing his space, and he looked over his shoulder to see yawning faces in the gray dawn. There would be breakfast once the horses were seen to. As Robbie attended to the new occupants of the stable, charming each with soft words, dry woolen blankets and a handful of oats, he felt new eyes upon him. He turned. In the doorway stood the most beautiful creature Rob had ever seen.

All of the stray thoughts that had led to the previous night's fantasy vanished, the visiting lord's rugged, golden beauty bleached into insignificance beside the smile that crinkled the corners of the deep brown eyes and upturned the edges of the deep pink lips on the face of this lady. Rob took a hesitant step forward and the horse he had been tending snorted and sidestepped and bumped him back into reality.

"So you're to be the new hostler?"

"The what now?" Rob said, watching the lady lean over the half door to pet the sturdy bay mare on the nose. Some of her ebony hair tumbled loose from its wrapping of indigo silk and he watched a spiral curl kiss her cheek.

"Hostler. The man who looks after our stable." She smiled at him. "My cousin spoke to you last night, yes? Offered you the position?"

"Last night? No. Maybe. I suppose I don't know," Robbie replied, head down, turning away and reaching for the bucket and shovel he'd rested against the wall while getting the animals accustomed to his movements. He started to scoop soiled straw into the bucket. The sturdy bay bumped him again and the lady laughed when Robbie cursed and sprawled.

"She's called Defiant for a reason," she said. "Let me distract her for you. My cousin's Friesian is called Darkness on account of his color, and the pony that's to be yours is called Sprite."

Rob raised an eyebrow and she laughed at his comical expression. "The position is vacant because she threw the last man as soon as his rump landed in the saddle two days back. He'll live, but he won't ride again soon. Sprite won't suffer to be ridden by anyone else since then. Perhaps she misses him."

The lady swung the half door open and came into the stall, not minding her fancy boots, and entertained Defiant by producing a shiny, red apple from a pocket and biting off chunks either to chew and eat herself or to offer up to Defiant's searching lips, once or twice having to hide the fruit and sternly tell the beast no when the mare went for the bigger prize in her other hand. Rob worked uncomfortably close beside her, trying his hardest to focus on the ill-mannered bay mare and not the ebony hair or the velvet black eyes or the smooth, brown cheek of the mare's mistress, or her scent that reminded him, in sweet wafts of lilac, of a warm summer evening with little to do but listen to the birds sing and the insects buzz and the leaves rustle.

The lady followed Rob out of the stall and smiled when he returned hauling clean straw, spreading some inside Defiant's stall while the mare watched him with mischief in her bearing. "Will you be taking her out today?" he asked, words rushed and eager, gut clenching at the thought he might be embarrassing himself. "I'll get her ready for you myself."

The lady did not respond, but she met Rob's nervous gaze with a raised eyebrow and another slight smile. "Did my cousin offer you the position or not?"

Rob sucked his lower lip and looked away for a few seconds as he tried to remember what the man had said. "A sandy-haired man spoke to me and said he might call on my services," he said, lifting the bucket. He dared to look at the lady's face again. "I did not know what he meant by that and he did not introduce himself. Perhaps it was someone else in your company. He looked not much like you, for a cousin."

She laughed and nodded. "That's him. Well. Will you be the new hostler or not? You're to leave here and travel with us."

"Leave here?" Rob felt like his heart might beat so hard it would wear out and stop like Da's.

"Yes." Her face fell. "Your Ma lives in the house and works the kitchen, I heard. Will you miss her so very much that you'd say no?"

Rob stood in silent thought, suddenly back by the old well with Ma, coins digging their edges into his palm. He gripped the handle of the bucket so hard that his forearms ached and his fingers whitened and tingled. He stood frozen for long enough that the lady turned to leave, but the glint of early morning sunlight from the clasp that secured her scarf over her hair brought him out of his trance and he called after her, "When do we leave?"

"Soon," she called back. "I'll send word."

Rob emerged from the stall where Defiant now tried to crush him against the wall. "Wait, please, Miss," he said. "I know your horses' names but not yours."

"Well," she said with a slight huff of a laugh. "You will call my cousin 'Sir' and you may call me 'My Lady'." She waited for Rob almost to catch up and gave him an appraising look. "I suppose I should have your name. My cousin calls everyone he considers beneath him 'Boy' but I think that won't do." Rob stood with his heart thumping and his stomach churning with apprehension about what the lady might say. "I won't call you Boy," she said, taking a step close, closer, too close, looking Rob up and down then frowning into his pink face and shaking her head. "It's not right for you. He said you claim to be eighteen. What's your name, man?"

"Rob—" Rob swallowed away the dryness clagging his mouth and fought the spinning sensation brought on by relief. "Robert Kerry, my lady."

She smiled and stepped away. "Well Robert Kerry. Get my horses ready."

Rob watched her leave, peering around the stable block until she was out of sight in the hubbub surrounding the House. Once she was gone, he took a deep breath and sighed out, "Yes, my lady."

Another of the stable boys laughed behind him. "You ought to set your sights lower and one day you'll actually find a nice girl willing to warm your cockles."

"You shut your trap," Rob replied with a good-humored wink. "We've got extra horses to see to. I'll take the bay mare. You can start with the Friesian, if you can reach that high."

As soon as he had a moment to spare, Rob gathered his scant

possessions into a canvas bag, cleaned himself up as best he could and jogged up to the back of the House. Not daring to set a muddy foot inside, he hollered through the door. A face peered out and a scullery maid Rob didn't know well told him to wait. A few minutes later, Ma came out with floury hands and a stained apron and hugged him tightly, her head barely reaching past his shoulder. "One of the footmen told the between-maid, and she told Gramma and Gramma told me. You're going up in the world, my prince! Fancy hostler to a fancy lord and lady!"

"Ma, I–"

"You'll need some things for the journey." Ma still held him tightly. "Someone'll bring you the clothes I kept and mended for you. There's some underthings I fixed too and a shirt and even a coat. I'll miss you, my lad."

Ma's words were spiked with bright cheer, but Rob felt her tremble. He set his forehead on hers for a minute, closed his eyes, then kissed her cheek. "My mind's not made up. I'll stay if you want."

"What?" Ma pushed him off but held him no further than arm's length. "See the world, Robbie. Let the world see you too, eh?" She let go and wiped her eyes with the heels of her hands, leaving flour on her cheek. "There's not much for you here."

"But who'll look out for you?" Rob asked.

Ma hiccupped and laughed but when she spoke her voice sounded low and thick. "Don't you give me that, Rob Kerry. I looked out for myself for years, then I looked out for your Da and then I looked out for you." She looked away and blinked rapidly, swiping the heels of her hands across her eyes again. Rob reached over and wiped the flour from her cheek. "No," Ma said. "I'll be fine, Robbie, but you'll have to promise to me you'll look out for yourself."

Rob walked beside Sprite for the first day because he'd found a thorn in her hide, worked right under the hair where the saddle should sit. He'd nipped it out with pliers and applied salve while two of the other lads held her as still as she would manage. It looked clean enough, but she wouldn't wear a saddle today. He spoke often to the beast and fancied that he understood the snorts and puffs he received as replies, although he would never confess this to his new companions. Sir and the Lady rode side by side where the road allowed it, and the whole party was escorted by a few uniformed soldiers and their captain, a man of around thirty years with eyes as deep as the Lady's although his face was paler with a cooler tone, and sleek black hair tied at the nape of his neck. The troopers went scouting a little ahead, mounted on Fell ponies like Rob's, to deter opportunistic thieves on the rough road. The breed was not what Rob expected for military horses, but the captain told him tersely that their modest stature and hardy nature made them able to withstand long days of trekking. The foot soldiers took watch at the rear. The men near Rob drifted off into occasional quiet murmurs about their own concerns. With little interest in the cost of ale and the challenge of finding casual, warm companionship in whichever rowdy inn or genteel manor house would host them next, Rob let his mind wander.

"Kerry!"

Rob's head jerked up to find his new mistress twisted in her saddle, watching him. "My Lady?" He replied, speeding to catch up, Sprite pulling back just enough to register her displeasure at the change in pace.

"When we stop tonight, you will put on a uniform," she said in an imperious voice. "I will not ride out with a man who looks like a tramp."

"Yes, My Lady." Rob looked down with embarrassment at the freshly-mended clothes that Ma had sent to the stables for him before he'd left. "These are the finest clothes I own."

"I don't doubt it," the Lady replied, turning to face forwards again and shaking her head, making the tight, black ringlets under the hem of her silk scarf bounce around her shoulders. "Eric, please make sure the new man is suitably dressed before we're seen somewhere that matters."

His lordship scoffed but nodded. Rob lagged behind with Sprite to share his silence.

The company traveled as far as daylight would allow. Sir Eric chose a good site and the foot-soldiers set up camp while Rob, the captain, and the troopers led the animals a little away where they would have grazing and water, hobbled them, and relieved them of their loads and saddles. While he was soothing Defiant with quiet words and small treats, a soldier dropped a pile of clothing and a blanket behind him, startling the mare and making her stamp and snort and shy away, flattening her ears.

"There's some supper here and these ought to fit, near enough," the man said. "Her Ladyship says to put them on. The blanket's for her horse, not for you. She said you're not to come up to the campfire, you're to stay with the horses and make sure they're all still here come sun-up. There ought to be ten."

"Nine," Rob corrected, counting off his fingers. "His Lordship's Friesian, Her Ladyship's crossbred bay, mine, the captain's and the scouts'... that's five Fell ponies, plus the two Galloways."

"So, you can count well enough," the soldier said with a laugh. "Shame. Me and the lads wanted to see what you'd look like, all frantic over a lost pony."

The soldier left to rejoin his companions by the campfire. Rob checked on the troopers' care of their own mounts, cooing at the long, inquisitive but suspicious faces that greeted him, adjusting hobbles just to be sure the ponies were comfortable and secure, then cooed to Defiant and fixed the blanket over her back while shoving her head away to avoid her clicking teeth. As twilight's warmth cooled and faded to night, Rob sat on a fallen trunk to examine the bundle. There was clothing but no food, and Rob's belly growled at the broken promise of being filled. He shook out a serviceable pair of faded gray breeches with only one darned tear, a blue jacket with brass buttons on the front and a small, ragged hole in the side, and a tunic that may once have been white but now had a hole to match the one in the jacket and a large but faint, tea colored stain around it. Clearly, Rob thought with a grimace, this uniform had not come cheaply from its previous owner.

"Robert Kerry."

The voice startled Rob and he whirled around to find its source. The Lady stood at the edge of the small clearing that allowed grass and ferns to shoot up to see who'd reach the sun first. Her corkscrew ringlets hung loose, and she shook them out with a hand before walking a few steps closer. She lowered her voice. "Did I get you all wrong? Before?" Rob's confusion must have shown on his face despite the meager moonlight, for she laughed quietly. "Maybe I did. I apologize for the haughty way I spoke to you about your clothes. My cousin has been lecturing me about how a noble Lady ought to speak to servants, but it does not come naturally." Rob thought he detected bitterness in the Lady's voice, but she shook it off. "I sent food, clothes, and a blanket so you could sleep away from the men. The other men. But I heard that donkey I sent with your bundle braying to his herd about breaking in the new boy." She looked Rob up and down again, eyes black in the scant twilight. "I am right, aren't I? You'd rather the other men not see you intimately?"

Rubber-kneed and nauseous, Rob swallowed and waited for his world to end. But the Lady's hand came out, holding a cloth parcel. "It's only bread, a little meat and some cheese from your ma's kitchen, and the apple I was saving to sweeten Defiant in the morning."

"Thank you," Rob said quietly, stepping close enough to take the offering, close enough to touch the fingers of her outstretched hand. "My Lady," he added when she arched an eyebrow and smiled.

"You look–" she said, then caught herself. "You look like a fine soldier."

Defiant chose that moment to totter over and nose at her mistress for attention. The Lady laughed aloud. "Your blanket, I presume?" She spoke gentle nonsense to her mare while untying the blanket, and the mare stood calmly. "I want you to be good for this one," she crooned. "I like him." Then she handed the blanket out to Rob and gave him a serious look. "I promise you have nothing to fear from me."

I like him. Three words, replayed over in his mind until he had the precise tone and timbre of her voice memorized and stored beside the warmth of her expression when she was alone with him, made Rob's pulse quicken and his head fill with possibilities. It was fully night, lit only by meager starlight, when Rob wrapped the blanket around himself and settled to sleep. In his fantasy, the face of the tall, soft-bearded man he had thought of as his savior from a life limited by the boundary stones of the land belonging to the House, was gradually replaced by jet black hair, high cheekbones over smooth cheeks, and deep, dark eyes. He lay awake with a smile as he imagined kissing first her hand, then her cheek, then her lips, but he forced his mind into blankness as his fingers satisfied his desire.

The next morning, woken by habit, birdsong and gray dawn light, Rob gathered his things and listened out for the soldiers stirring and wanting to wash in the shallow stream too. He checked on the horses and counted them as he made his way to the water's edge. As he was finishing, two of the foot soldiers rattled and swore their way down to the water with empty canteens swinging from their arms. Rob brought the horses one by one closer to the small camp and glanced across to the Lady's little tent as he checked over Sprite's hide for signs of healing. Sprite allowed it without complaint but there was no sign of life yet from the Lady. He set to Darkness first, befriending the huge beast with soft words, scratches on the neck, and chunks of the apple he'd saved from his supper in case breakfast wasn't made for him. Defiant was next and he laughed at the mare's impish sidestepping to try to bully him. He'd spared a chunk of apple for her reward too, but he snatched his fingers back the instant the mare bared her teeth. Defiant's loss was Rob's gain. He chewed the apple in front of her while she blew at him (indignantly, he fancied) then he moved on to Sprite instead.

A laugh made Rob look up from his careful study of Sprite's

injury. "You seem to have the measure of my mare," the Lady said, walking over and stroking Defiant fondly, feeding her from an open palm.

Rob smiled and blushed and looked away. "She'll learn, maybe. Probably," he added. "She doesn't bite you, my Lady, so she can't be all evil."

The lady gave a scornful little huff. "She remembers kindnesses. She hates my cousin. He used the whip to sting her into speed three days back and she's neither forgiven nor forgotten." Rob raised his eyebrows but said nothing. "You disapprove?" the Lady asked, coming around to look at whatever held Rob's attention.

Rob pointed out the healing injury site in Sprite's hide. He shrugged. "If you get a horse that likes sport, use it for sport. If you get one that doesn't, use it for another purpose. But if you take a horse that's unwilling and require it to perform tasks it hates, you're going to end up as the unsatisfied owner of an unhappy beast."

The lady's hand touched Rob's where it rested on Sprite's warm back for a moment and their eyes met. This time it was the Lady who looked away first. "Selene," she said quietly. "When it's just you and me and the animals, I would like you to call me Selene."

"Selene," Rob repeated quietly. Selene looked up again, smiled and turned to walk away.

The captain and his troopers set off ahead while the foot soldiers packed up the camp and loaded the horses. Sir Eric checked Rob's work and gave him a satisfied nod before seating himself on Darkness and watching as Rob crouched in front of Lady Selene and offered his clasped hands to help her mount. When Selene graciously accepted, putting one heel into Rob's hands and one hand on Rob's shoulder to steady herself as she swung up into her saddle, Sir Eric frowned until Selene dismissed Rob with a word and a flick of her hand. To Rob's relief, since his legs were stiff and aching from a full day of walking, Sprite consented to be saddled and ridden. As before, Selene rode with Eric and Rob brought up the rear with the pack animals. They set a sedate pace for the morning then stopped to let the horses rest while the humans stretched and sat and rummaged in saddlebags for bread and cheese. Rob and one of the troopers treated each animal to a meager handful of grain to supplement their overnight grazing, and the trooper murmured a promise to one pony in particular that there would be an inn tonight with a clean stable for the pony and a soft bunk for himself.

The afternoon stretched on as long as the road ahead of them when they set off again. Rob realized that Lady Selene had dropped back from her cousin's side and that he was catching her up. When Sprite drew level, he looked over and Selene smiled at him. "Do you need anything?" Rob asked. "Is Defiant all right?"

Sir Eric looked back and stopped Darkness to wait. Lady Selene pulled a face. "I think she is uncomfortable. Perhaps when we stop next you will check her over."

"Stop and see to it now, boy," Sir Eric called out. "Quickly. The lady will ride your pony. You can catch up."

"Yes, sir," Rob said, slipping from his saddle and landing on his feet. He walked over to Selene and held his hand up. "My lady?"

Selene gave Rob an imperious glare but allowed him to help her safely to the ground. Partly hidden by Defiant's brown flank, she shrugged at Rob and murmured an apology. "I hoped he'd let us stop and examine her together. There's nothing wrong."

"Selene?" Sir Eric called over in exasperation.

"Coming," Selene called back. "Please check her rear leg. Here."

Selene cooed at Defiant and patted her as she moved. Rob followed. As they both ducked to feel the firm muscle and bone of Defiant's leg, faces barely an inch apart, Rob felt warm breath on his skin and the slightest of pressure from Selene's lips on his cheek. Rob took a sharp breath in and held it, feeling his pulse speed up, then turned to see Selene's face, but she had stepped away immediately, leaving Rob wondering if that ghost of a kiss had merely been wishful thinking. With her back to Rob, Selene swung herself onto Sprite and trotted to catch up to her cousin.

Rob pushed Defiant's head away with a stern *no!* when the mare tried to groom his shoulder, then checked over her hind legs while she was distracted by a clump of lush grass just off the road. It gave him time to think about what had happened, if it had really happened at all. Perhaps he had imagined a kiss on his cheek. Perhaps, he told himself, it was normal for Lady Selene to thank someone with a kiss, although he had not seen her kiss Sir Eric. Perhaps it was an accident because they were so close together.

"Defiant," he said to the mare, rubbing her neck. "Did you bump your mistress into me?"

Defiant, of course, did not reply. He walked her for a while to get a feel for her gait before urging her into a trot. He caught up to the little traveling group quickly since they had stopped to rest only a couple of miles further on. He presented himself to Lady Selene with his stomach churning and his head spinning just a little.

"My Lady," he said, then cleared his throat. "My Lady, I examined your mare thoroughly and—"

"This had better not all be for no reason," Sir Eric butted in sharply, directing a scowl at Selene. "There have been far too many delays on this journey."

Selene turned her attention to Rob, eyebrows raised and lower lip caught, a flash of pink between white teeth. "I am sure if there was a problem, your new man *will have found it.*"

Rob detected a slight emphasis on Selene's last few words. He wetted his lips. "Um, yes. There was a thorn. I have removed it and she seems happier."

Sir Eric huffed. "That beast is never happy."

Selene mouthed thank you when her cousin looked away. "Well then," she said aloud. "We can set off as soon as you have her ready for me."

Rob nodded and trotted away to prepare the animals for the next stage of the journey. The captain was about to set off ahead once more, already mounted and waiting for his troopers. He nodded a greeting to Rob. "You're good with the animals."

Rob nodded back. "Started as a stable lad as soon as I was tall enough to hold a shovel."

The captain laughed. "And I joined the dragoons as soon as I could lift my grandfather's sword without falling over. Like the other men here, I served my time and work privately now. Are you staying on as Sir Eric's man, or Lady Selene's?"

"What do you mean?" Rob asked with a frown wrinkling his brow. "I thought we were going…"

It hit Rob like a breaking wave over his head that he had no idea where the party was headed, or why, other than *away* and *because we can*.

"Oh! Of course you're new." The captain clicked at his pony who was restless and ready to move. "Sir Eric is escorting his cousin to her wedding. We have another three or four days' journey, if the good weather holds." The captain gave in to his pony's demand to move. "At least there's an inn tonight," he called over his shoulder, "so the men will have beer and company to cheer them up."

Frowning, Rob led both Defiant and Darkness over to their mistress and master. Sir Eric mounted with barely a grunt of thanks. Lady Selene smiled at Rob then frowned back at his lack of response. They set off after the mounted guardsmen, with Sir Eric in front, then Lady Selene, four foot-soldiers and two pack horses, then Rob.

Lost in thought, Rob let Sprite follow at her own pace. Of course Lady Selene did not admire him. Of course she was to marry someone noble and have a happy life with a man of her own standing. Of course he was a fool to entertain even a fantasy that Lady Selene wanted anything from him other than his skill with the horses. He plodded along thinking of Ma and Gramma and his stables, wondering if the lads were taking proper care of old Silver and if Henry had replaced him yet. He considered letting the party get further ahead then turning Sprite around and following the road back. Back to Ma, back to questions about why he'd come back so soon before giving himself a chance to get to know the world and before giving the world a chance to get to know him. Back to confess shamefacedly to Henry and the lads that he'd followed a girl and it hadn't worked out. No, he thought grimly. He'd forget about Lady Selene. Surely her new husband would have his own stable master, and he'd be returning with the gruff Sir Eric, letting his memory of Selene fade into nothing. He'd be better off on his own. Decision made, Rob allowed himself a few more minutes to calm his turbulent emotions. Once he was sure he would not weep or rage with either sadness, disappointment, or anger at himself, he urged Sprite to trot and caught up.

The rest of the day's travel passed quietly. The soldiers appeared to be playing some kind of word game, too quiet for Rob to figure out exactly how the game worked and certainly too quietly for Sir Eric to hear. He considered hanging back a little, maybe walking and leading Sprite so that he could ask to join in, but as soon as he looked back at them the soldiers paused their game and looked around as if vigilant for attack from the rear. No matter, he thought. He could try making friends with the soldiers later, perhaps over supper at the inn. Once at the inn, however, Rob's time was occupied with stabling Defiant and Darkness, and seeing that the Fell ponies and the Galloways were secure in the paddock and had sufficient grazing and water as well as an extra portion of grain to make up for their long day of walking. The troopers helped out with their own mounts before disappearing into the inn, leaving Rob alone to finish his tasks. As he was departing the stable yard, belongings in a bag over his shoulder, contemplating the soft amber light that glowed in the narrow windows and frowning at the harsh laughter and off-key songs that came from the doorway, Sir Eric walked over, nodding in greeting. Rob wondered if he ought to bow. "Sir Eric," he said. "Would you like to see how well Darkness looks after a brushing?"

"That's not necessary, I trust your work, boy. Lady Selene has arranged out of her own purse for you and her captain to share a private room instead of bunking with the other men."

Rob's eyebrows shot up in surprise. "That is very kind of her. Please will you tell the Lady thank you from me?"

"I am sure she can hear it from you herself tomorrow," Sir Eric said, already turning away. "Are you a drinker? There's ale."

"No, sir!" Rob called after his employer.

Sir Eric paused and looked round at Rob with an approving nod. "Then come inside, boy."

Rob followed a minute after Sir Eric, into light and warmth and noise, and sat at the end of a long table claimed by the other men. Sir Eric was not to be seen, and neither was Lady Selene. Rob asked the soldier beside him if the Lady had eaten yet and the man shrugged. Someone brought him a bowl of stew and a chunk of bread and Rob ate voraciously, barely noticing when the men all shuffled up, someone produced playing cards, and the group embarked on a drinking game. The straw-haired, rosy-cheeked girl who had brought his meal over came to take his dishes, then returned with a second portion for him. Instead of slipping silently away to attend to other patrons, she slipped into the seat opposite Rob and rested her chin on her hands.

"You're a handsome one," she said brightly, blinking her blue eyes at him. "Better looking than your mates, here. What's your name, sweet?"

Rob almost choked on his stew. "Rob," he said hoarsely, coughing. The girl laughed.

"Well, Rob, I'm Emmie," she said, reaching over to pat his cheek. "Ask for me if you're lonely later."

With that, Emmie got up and wandered over to another table. Rob finished his meal and watched the game for a few minutes. The men were taking turns revealing a pair of cards and whoever got the highest score had to drink. The seat opposite him scraped again and the captain sat down. "Want to join in?" he asked. Rob shook his head. "Good man, very wise." The captain looked over at where Emmie was flirting with another guest. "Wise enough not to sup from that tankard either, I hope."

Rob must have gone bright red for he felt a flare of heat in his cheeks and the captain laughed. "No."

"Just as well, I expect she'll be busy enough tonight. Now, you and I have a private room to share, but I always sleep where my men do. Partly because it's fairer and partly because they will be better behaved if they know I am going to witness any drunkenness."

"They are drinking now," Rob said, pointing as one of the men turned over two jacks and all but the man who had played cheered, slapped the table, and took a drink each.

"They are," the captain admitted. "But with this game, unless someone plays a pair only the highest score earns a drink so they could play all night and barely sup enough each to make them merry."

Rob watched the next round. The first man pulled a total of ten. The second scored twelve and the first threw down his cards and cursed in disgust. Rob laughed. "What's your name?"

"Thomas Mallock," the captain said, offering a handshake. "I'm Lady Selene's man."

"Robert Kerry," Rob said, accepting it. Despite his earlier resolve, he felt the dull ache of disappointment. He tried to keep his voice low and even. "What do you mean you're Lady Selene's man?"

Mallock smiled and cocked an eyebrow. "Nothing for Sir Eric to be concerned about if that's what you mean. I'm appointed by her mother to see that the Lady is safely wed and to act as her protector should anything unfortunate happen on the journey." Mallock cheered along as one of his men pulled a score of seventeen. "I'm glad Sir Eric employed you. Otherwise, we'd be down both a man and a maid and I'd have care of the horses. I swear that bay mare hates everyone except milady."

"Down a man and a maid?" Rob asked, suddenly wary of the captain's friendliness.

"As it happens, it was milady's girl the man was after, not Selene herself. When he was thrown from your pony, she left her position to care for him." Captain Mallock grinned. "I expect they will be happy together now they have no need for sneaking around. Lady Selene wept at losing her. She treated her maid more like a sister than a servant. Sir Eric disapproved." Mallock waved at his men to deal him into the next game. "I suppose women are like that," he said, peeking at his cards and shaking his head. "Well, Kerry," Captain Mallock played his hand to good natured jeers from his men, "your beasts are safely settled for the night so you should do likewise. Mine are not, so I will stay up and regret it come morning."

Rob smiled and stood. "My beasts take longer to get ready, so I'll take your advice. Goodnight."

Rob took his bag, climbed the narrow staircase, and walked across the creaky wooden floorboards of a passage bordered by three doors on the left and five on the right. The first on the right was wide open so he went inside. The room was tiny but clean with bedding that smelled fresh although it had seen better days, and the small, unglazed, square window looked out over the stable yard. From here, Rob could see the faint glow of a lamp in the loft of the stable. He wondered with a sudden pang of longing if the lads back home had brought old Silver in from the paddocks and if they'd thanked Ma properly for their meals. Rob blamed the hot prickle under his eyelids on the pollen in the night air, but left the shutters open anyway. He closed the door, stripped and washed in the basin provided with cold water from a jug, did his best to launder his underclothes and draped them to dry across the window like curtains. He slipped between the sheets wearing his old shirt, the one Lady Selene had scorned. As he drifted into sleep, his thoughts were filled with the scent of Ma's bread and fresh hay, and the sounds of the lads chattering about nothing.

It wasn't gray light through the window or the sound of the innkeeper's chickens that roused Rob. He lay in darkness, moonlight seeping into the room, and listened. There! The noise came again. A creak, a knock, a laugh and a soft call of, "it's only me, sweet," and a low, harsh, reply of "hush." Rob sat up and put one foot on the floor but waited. Another creak, then the sharp click of a latch closing. The next laugh was muffled. Rob sighed, pulling his leg back into bed and lay down, hoping that Emmie at least had a pleasant night with whichever patron asked for her. A minute later, a soft knock came at Rob's door. He froze, watching as his door opened a few inches. A quiet voice, pitched low, called through the gap. "Are you awake, Robert Kerry?"

Rob eased out of bed and padded to the door. He opened it slowly, stopping as soon as he heard the slightest squeak from the hinges. "I'm awake."

He stepped back and Selene slipped into his room, closing the door softly behind her. "Sorry to wake you," she murmured, smiling. "My cousin is entertaining a guest. He'll be occupied for a while."

"Emmie? The serving lass?" Rob's eyes widened. "Sir Eric–"

"Hush!" Selene's smile widened into a grin. "I paid her to take her time with him."

Rob's hands flew to his flaming cheeks. "She offered me... Never mind."

Selene shook with stifled laughter. "Were you tempted? Do you like girls, Robert?"

"Rob," Rob said, blood rushing in his ears. "Call me Rob."

"Well, Rob, do you?"

Rob's heart thumped in his ribcage and the rush of blood made his limbs feel loose. Mouth dry, he sucked at his lower lip and tried to swallow before he spoke. "Some," he said, hesitantly. "I like some girls."

"Oh," Selene said, cocking an eyebrow. "Tell me about the girls you like, Rob."

"You ought not to be here, my lady," Rob said, words tumbling over each other. "You're on your way to be wed."

Selene's face fell into a deep scowl and her next words hissed with suppressed fury. "And you of all people remind me of my place in the world! You might as well have slapped me. It would have stung less."

Rob took a half step forward, hands out, palms up. Selene stepped back. "Don't you want that?" Rob asked. "To marry a lord or a prince or whoever he is?"

"To be escorted under guard, far away from home, to promise to please a stranger until it's decided he has enough heirs?" Selene's voice turned harsh. "Would you want that, Rob? I thought I might find some sympathy from you." She took a breath in and held it for a few seconds, then let it out slowly. Rob saw that her fists were clenched tight around the fabric of her long nightgown. "Even Emmie the serving lass has choice. If she hadn't liked Eric's handsome face she could've told me no. But I had no say in this." Shoulders sagging, Selene covered her face. Rob wrapped his arms around her. She rested her head on his shoulder, arms slipping around his waist. "At least let me have these few days with a friend at my side."

"A friend," Rob said, turning his head to breathe in the sweet lilac scent of her hair. "Of course I will be your friend." Rob thought of the light brush of Selene's lips against his cheek from earlier and he pressed a dry kiss to her temple. Selene raised her head, smoothed Rob's hair back from his eyes, then smiled and kissed his lips.

"So tell me, Rob," she said quietly, "about the girls you like."

"Girl," Rob whispered, heart pounding so hard he was sure she'd feel it too. "I like just one girl."

Rob felt like the world halted its dance through the heavens and only he kept spinning when Selene kissed him again, one hand in his hair and the other around his waist. He copied whatever she did as best he could, fingers brushing Selene's curls, lips parting, the tip of his tongue teasing hers, his body pressed against hers in a way that coaxed a familiar dull throb between his legs, and a fierce heat bloomed his throat and face.

"Selene," he said, lips moving against hers.

"I want this." She guided Rob's hand from her hair to the swell of her breast. "Lie with me."

"I've not—"

"Have you never given a woman pleasure, Robert Kerry?"

Rob shook his head. "Nor a man."

"What about your own pleasure?" Selene asked. Rob held his breath as his gaze met hers. He slowly nodded. "Don't you want to?" she asked, and he nodded again. Selene grinned and led him to his bed. "Then I think you know where to start."

He'd been told years ago that he'd just know what to do when his first time came, but uncertainty struck like the paralyzing bite from a viper. Selene lay back, took his hands and placed them on her breasts, asked for a kiss. At the sight of her shining eyes, something unlocked inside him and a flood of ideas about what he might do inundated Rob's imagination. He sat astride her thighs, cupped her breasts, thumbs feeling for the hard pucker of her nipples, ducked to kiss them through her linen nightdress, then pushed the loose fabric up so that he could kiss her warm skin. Selene tried to return the favor, but Rob gently moved away and kissed her palm. He stroked her smooth belly and trailed fingers through the soft, thick hair between her legs, marveling wordlessly at the warm wetness there, kissing Selene's mouth again while his fingertips rubbed back and forth. Selene stretched, opened her mouth wider, tensed her legs under Rob and her breathing became a few seconds of shallow, rapid panting, then she sighed, clung to Rob and laughed.

They turned to lie side by side, facing each other. Selene stroked Rob's face. "I want to touch you like that too," she said. "Will you let me?" Rob barely moved. Selene ran her free hand over his shirt to rest on his hip. Rob put his hand on top of Selene's. "Don't you want to?"

"I don't know," Rob said. "Is that bad? From their talk, the stable lads all seemed to want it all the time, but I never felt like that."

"Are you saying you don't want to?"

"I'm saying I don't know if I want to or not, or even what I want."

"What if I touch you," she said gently, pausing to kiss his lips, "and if you like it I'll keep going and if you don't I'll stop."

Rob said nothing more, but released Selene's hand. He lay still, closed his eyes and felt Selene's cool fingers slide under the hem of his shirt. But he froze when a loud, muffled groan and an even louder, higher moan of pleasure came from one of the other rooms. Selene sighed and got up, shaking her nightgown into place.

"That's Emmie's signal. I have to go back to my room."

"Oh." Rob stood up too, following Selene to the door in a daze. "Goodnight, then."

Selene paused with the door open, peered out then turned and kissed Rob one last time before slipping away. Rob watched with one eye at the door, open a mere crack now, until Selene let herself safely back into her own room opposite his. A few minutes later, lying with his eyes closed and the memory of the feel of Selene's body under his, Rob heard one of the bedroom doors squeak open and bang closed, then footsteps creaking down the staircase.

Chickens clucking and squawking in the yard under his window woke Rob from a sleep that felt both too deep and too brief. He dressed quickly, slurped down a bowl of thin oatmeal at the same table he'd occupied last evening, then went out to see to his duties. He had almost finished before he caught sight of Selene, across the stable yard.

"Kerry!" she called to him, frowning. Rob's stomach fluttered and his heart sped up a little although faint dread tempered his excitement at seeing her.

"In here," he called. "Just getting her saddled for you."

"About time," she snapped as she walked into the stable block, looking this way and that. Rob watched, waiting to find out whether he should smile or not. "Are there no other stable lads here to help you?"

"No, Lady Selene. They've gone inside for breakfast."

Selene looked left and right one more time, then over her shoulder back out of the stable door, then grinned. "Kiss me good morning, love," she said, leaning over the half door of the stall to watch him adjust Defiant's saddle. "Did you sleep well?"

Rob laughed. "After you left, I thought I would never sleep again, but I went out like a snuffed candle."

Selene raised her eyebrows. "Oh? Did you dream of me?"

"I–" Rob smiled. "I did. Of course."

"I bet you did not. Come here, you liar."

Rob walked across the stall with Defiant's reins, the horse following. Selene put a hand on his cheek then reached to kiss him. Rob leaned in, eyes closed, the warmth of the kiss bringing back the familiar heavy, insistent feeling low in his groin. He pulled back and groaned softly. "Today is going to be torture. Seeing you up ahead and knowing what you face."

"We have to be careful, Rob. Eric can't know or he'll get rid of you."

Rob nodded. "I will. I'll—"

Someone coughed from the main door of the stables. Selene sprang back from the stall and Rob ducked behind Defiant. "You need to be more careful than that," Captain Mallock said as he approached. "You know I'll say nothing, but others might tattle in the hope of an extra few coins from your cousin. He sent me to fetch you. He's anxious to get moving."

The day progressed much as the previous one had, with Captain Mallock and his men riding a little ahead, Sir Eric and Lady Selene next, then Rob leading the pack horses so that the foot soldiers could look out for all the potential dangers of the road. But today Rob stole covert glances at Selene, and she turned to seek him out and smile whenever Sir Eric's attention was taken. When they stopped to let the horses rest, Rob was careful not to appear too attentive. When they were ready to set off again, he still offered, "Hand up, milady?" but kept his head down as Selene tucked her foot into his clasped hands and hoisted herself into the saddle.

The whole party caught up to Captain Mallock at a farmhouse when the sun had slipped enough to slant through the trees. "Sir Eric," Mallock called as he walked over, leading his pony. "The farmer can sell us provisions and accommodate us if you and Lady Selene are looking for a comfortable night. There's no inn at the marketplace any more on account of a fire."

Sir Eric tutted and scowled. He looked up at the pale blue sky shaded by light gray clouds. "No," he said after a short deliberation. "Take the provisions if the food looks good, but we keep going. If we don't reach the next village or inn or manor by nightfall, we'll pitch the tents and make do. Tell your men to look out for a suitable campsite."

"Yes, sir," Mallock said with a curt nod. He got back on his pony and trotted off to relay their new orders.

"You don't mind, do you?" Sir Eric said to Selene, turning and catching her exchanging smiles with Rob. "A few more hours of travel today might make up for some of your delays earlier in the journey. Save the embarrassment of arriving late to your own wedding."

The group met up again as evening colors faded into twilight. The foot soldiers set about making camp while Mallock and Rob led the animals through the trees to find water and grazing. Rob chose his own spot for the night, private enough except for the occasional, inquisitive, equine nose, within sight of the campfire and sound of the soldiers' banter, then ventured closer to the main camp to collect his share of food. This time, Mallock called him over and made space for him, and he watched the men play a noisy game of cards that seemed to have rules which changed when the players saw fit.

As the night air cooled and stars winked here and there, Sir Eric, never far from Lady Selene's shoulder, declared it time to rest and sent Selene to her tent. "Kerry!" one of the soldiers called. In the faint light Rob recognized the man who had tried pranking him on his first night. "You sleeping by the embers with the rest of us?"

"No," Rob said, angling his head in the direction of the hobbled mounts. "With them."

"I said he's not allowed," Mallock added. "Have you heard him snore? Brays like a smacked mule."

A couple of the soldiers laughed and one asked if he smelled like one too, but soon the banter drifted away from Rob. He answered Mallock's wink with a grin and slipped off to wash and sleep in silver moonlight and solitude.

When Rob returned from sluicing the day's dust and sweat from his skin at the little pond from which the horses had drunk, a blanket-shrouded figure was waiting for him. From her height and the way she moved, Rob recognized Selene before he could see her beautiful face.

"We need to be careful!" Rob said as quiet as the whisper of water from the stream that fed the pond.

"I was. I waited until he was asleep, then I waited a bit longer." Selene reached a hand to Rob and he clasped it between both of his. "I wanted to see you. Give me something good to dream about."

Rob smiled and looked around the blacks and grays of the woodland at night, but the trees and shrubs stood guard impassively. A loud pop and crackle from the embers of the camp-fire startled him and Selene suppressed a giggle at his nervous jump. Around them, some of the horses tore up mouthfuls of the lush grass that grew in thick tussocks wherever there were gaps in the canopy while others lay or rolled, snorting and snoring. Rob breathed out a laugh. "What did you have in mind?"

Selene did not reply. She moved closer to Rob, and kissed him. He wrapped his arms around her and returned the kiss, feeling the press of Selene's body against his and imagining how it might feel were there no layers of linen and wool between them. "Come over here," she murmured in his ear, leading him to the trunk of one of the more mature trees bordering the ragged little clearing, faced away from camp. "Let's pretend there's only us here. Only us in the whole world."

Rob leaned his back against the bumpy bark of the linden tree and Selene leaned against him for another kiss. "Only us? Is that what you want to dream about?"

"This." Selene ran her hand down the front of Rob's shirt, slipping cool fingers inside and playing with the ribbon of his bodice. "I want to dream of you and me."

Selene kissed Rob again with parted lips, her hand drifting lower to unfasten the cord and buttons that held his breeches up. Torn between want and fear of discovery, Rob gave in to desire and shifted one arm down around Selene's waist, holding her closer, kissing her deeply, his free hand cupping the swell of her breast through far too many layers.

"I want to touch you like you touched me," Selene murmured. "Will you let me?"

Rob's head bumped against the bark behind him as Selene's fingers slipped further down to brush over the springy hair between his thighs. "Yes," he whispered, then let his eyes fall shut.

Afterwards, Rob held Selene in his arms, smiling softly. "It's better with you," he said. "More–"

"What do you mean?" Selene replied indignantly, pushing away from him. "I thought you said you hadn't been with a woman or a man before!"

"No!" Rob said, laughing. "I said that all wrong. I meant it's better with you than on my own. More… Just more. I don't have the words for it."

Selene snorted and cuffed Rob lightly on the head. "Faint praise indeed!"

"What will we do when we arrive?"

"I don't want to think about it," Selene sighed, leaning into Rob. "I was almost reconciled with the idea of living an obedient life as a good lady wife because that's what I've always been told I must do. I was taught that everyone must follow the path set out for them. Then I met Miss Coira at your old manor and found out that her father has promised that she may marry any hard-working man of good honor she chooses, or even remain unwed. And I thought, if this country mistress can choose her path, why can't I? If she can decide whether or not to produce heirs to inherit some landowner's estate, why can't I?"

"Miss Coira," Rob said with a smile. "I bet she'll marry a farmer soon and make a half-dozen happy little farmer babies to cluck over."

Selene shuddered. "That's not for me. And then I met you, Rob, and you struck me dizzy with hope that I might make my own path too. Only I can't think of how."

They leaned into each other for another minute then murmured their goodnights. Rob watched Selene pick her way through the sparse shrubs towards the main camp. A twig snap to his left caught Rob's attention. He turned to peer into the gloom. "Is that you spooking me, Defiant?" he asked, but there was no answering snort or groan or nicker, so he wrapped up in his blanket and lay down to sleep.

When he woke, it was to the sensation of a heavy fist pulling him upright by the blanket that wrapped and pinned his arms. "It seems my cousin likes you." The voice was a threatening murmur, breath ghosted hot across his ear. "Why are you special to her, I wonder." Rob froze. Rough stubble scratched at his cheek and his lungs heaved for want of air. Pale gray pre-dawn light lent an eerie glow to the mist that rose from the pond, glinted around ink-black pupils and turned pale straw hair to iron. Rob could neither move to help himself nor shout out for aid. His arms and legs were caught up in the blanket and when he opened his mouth to beg Sir Eric to leave him alone, the hand that sealed his lips pressed even harder and he tasted the coppery tang of blood on his tongue. "Don't make a sound," the man growled low, like a wolf come after a foal. "I'll treat you like the last man if I find out you spoiled her for her husband."

The grip on Rob's mouth eased and he had the briefest second to take a gasping breath in before the hand clamped around his throat. Rob cried out once, voice hoarse, unable to form words. From the direction of the pond, Rob heard Darkness whinny and an answer from one or two of the ponies, and closer in he heard snorts and huffs. Twigs crackled and hooves thumped. A dark shape loomed out of the morning fog. Rob recognized Defiant by her size and her bearing and the gait that showed she'd got free of her hobble. Sir Eric twisted his grip on Rob's blanket, lifted him clear off his feet and pushed him up against the same linden tree where he'd spent precious, joyful minutes with Selene. "I haven't–" he said, but Sir Eric cut his words off with a sudden, loud bellow.

"You dare? To answer me?"

Startled, Defiant reared up and crashed down behind Sir Eric then skittered away. Head spinning and throat aching, Rob Kerry fell winded to the cold, damp earth, trying to make sense of the noise and confusion in his head. The hulking form of Sir Eric lay prone with his head against one of the gnarly, protruding roots of the tree. Rob scrabbled free of his blanket and pushed himself up, but dark swirling shapes swarmed his vision. His head swam, his ears rang loud inside his head and he fell.

Rob came to his senses surrounded by a commotion of shouting and alarm. "Get up, man! Did you see what happened?" One of the soldiers held out his hand. Rob took it, hauling himself up, fighting the gray that fogged his head and letting out a groan.

"No. I was out cold," he admitted, voice hoarse.

Sir Eric lay unmoving. One soldier slowly walked towards him and the others backed away. One of them pointed at Rob. "What have you done?"

"Nothing!" Rob said, closing his eyes to conjure up an event maybe only minutes in the past. "He came to ask – I woke up with him – his hands–" He broke off and touched his neck where bruises would blossom purple and blue soon. "He accused me of–" Rob tried again but the right words would not come. His legs folded. He sat on the cold ground and wept.

"Sir Eric is injured!" the first guard cried out. The second remained over Rob, hand on the hilt of his sword ready for action should Rob have the strength or the will to fight or flee. Some of the other men grumbled at having been woken before they were ready but almost all came to gawk.

Rob sat with his arms around his knees. Captain Mallock picked up his blanket and draped it over his shoulders. As the sky lightened into true morning, a voice broke through Rob's walls and a face appeared level with his. "What happened?"

Rob blinked and raised his eyes to look at Selene. "He wanted to know if we–" Rob said quietly. "He came to–"

"Hush," she said, a hand gentle on his shoulder. "Not in front of the men. Did you try to kill him for it?"

"No!"

"Well then," Selene said a little louder. "There's no reason for them to accuse you." She looked up at the man standing guard over Rob. "Stand down, man. Take me to see my cousin."

Rob watched as Selene knelt beside Sir Eric for several minutes. Behind him, he could hear the bustle of the soldiers preparing breakfast and, nearby, the snorts and huffs of the horses. Selene leaned in and examined her cousin's injuries closely. Eventually she called for Captain Mallock.

"What do you think?" she said loudly enough for Rob to hear. "There's not much blood. Kicked by a horse?"

"Perhaps, my lady," Mallock said. Rob looked up and saw Selene watching him. Mallock stepped closer to Sir Eric. "Looks like it clipped his skull. I've seen men recover from worse, but not often. He'll need careful handling and proper care for some time to come."

Selene turned a thoughtful frown onto Rob then addressed Captain Mallock again. "We should see him cared for. Will you move him into the warmth and send out your men to find the nearest competent surgeon?"

Mallock called for his troopers and the foot soldiers. Two of the troopers he ordered to catch and saddle their ponies and ride to the next town, then return with a doctor. The foot soldiers he ordered to take care of Sir Eric. Under his direction, Rob watched them construct a stretcher from two stout poles and canvas from one of the tents. With great care to pull together, all six remaining soldiers lifted Sir Eric onto the stretcher and carried him closer to the fire. That done, Captain Mallock pointed at Rob. "You there! Kerry the hostler! Tend the horses. We'll remain here until the surgeon comes."

Shaking himself out of his torpor, Rob stood and stamped life and warmth back into his feet. His neck ached and his ribs felt like a hay bale had been dropped on him, but he was grateful that Mallock had set him to work. He strung a rope between the sturdy lower branches of two neighboring trees and starting with Darkness, one by one he brought the horses up and tethered them, untying their hobbles so that they could move more freely but could be quickly caught and readied for travel. Defiant was last. He rattled a few handfuls of grain in a pail as he searched around the pond and a little way into the woodland and the clearing beyond it until she wandered over, nickering at him in anticipation of treats and without the slightest care that the soft cord that had restricted her movement trailed frayed ends on the ground.

By the time he returned to the camp, two more men were absent, sent by Selene to take a letter to her future husband, informing him that the party would arrive a day or two late. Rob approached the camp-fire where Sir Eric lay unconscious and Selene sat with a frown. Captain Mallock and the soldiers alternated between tending the camp, playing games, and checking that Sir Eric was still breathing. Rob sat on the ground near Selene. "I'm sorry about your cousin," he said. "Defiant broke her hobble. When Sir Eric shouted at me, she was right behind him and–"

"I know," Selene said sharply, then her features softened. "I wish none of this had happened. I wish Eric had never known that he had a cousin from a family with deep connections but shallow coffers. I wish he had never been in the service of a man with an interest in bloodlines more appropriate for breeding horses. And I wish I had half of your courage not to accept the life set out for me."

"Hush," Rob said, squeezing Selene's hand. "Wishes can't change the past."

It was mid-afternoon before the troopers sent to fetch a surgeon returned, walking their ponies one either side of a horse and cart driven by a young man of no more than Rob's age and carrying a spare-built, gray-haired, man who introduced himself as an army surgeon, now retired from duty but serving quietly as the town's medical man. The surgeon examined Sir Eric and ordered him to be laid as carefully as possible on his cart. "I've seen injuries like this before. I can only see that he is cared for until he wakes from this coma," the surgeon said to Captain Mallock. "I have a private sickroom available. To whom should I send his account?"

Rob's head whipped round to glare at the doctor for such an insensitive intrusion as to ask about money when a man's life was uncertain. But Selene grabbed his arm tightly and he bit back the words he might have said. "To my husband and his master, Lord Crawford," she said. "Would you agree to take one of the ponies as part payment in advance? I can send two of his men to act as his nurses so that your other patients will not suffer."

The surgeon looked at the Fell ponies ridden by the troopers and nodded. "Aye, if it's a strong one and accustomed to a harness."

"Milady?" Captain Mallock said. "The Fell ponies are only used to the saddle. One of the Galloways would be best suited. Do you agree, Kerry?"

Rob looked up at Mallock and the surgeon, chewing his lip. Like him, the troopers got to know and respect their mounts and losing one of the Fell ponies would be a blow for whichever of the men had to give his away. "Yes," he said, scrambling to his feet and giving Mallock a curt nod. "I'll fetch them and the doctor can choose."

On the promise of a fortnight's pay in advance, a clean bunk in a warm sickroom and hot food every night, the two remaining foot soldiers agreed to accompany their master. Lady Selene drew herself up to her full height and instructed them imperiously not to leave Sir Eric's side, but to see that he was well cared for and to send word as soon as he showed any hint of recovery. Rob watched the surgeon check over the Galloways, ending with a nod and a satisfied hum as he chose one.

The surgeon's cart rumbled slowly away. The traveling party, reduced to Lady Selene, Rob, Mallock and his three troopers, sat around the fire more for the illusion of cheer than for the warmth it gave. "We could pack up camp and move on," Mallock said, staring into the flames. "But we might not reach an inn before dark." He looked over the flames at Selene. "It's your decision, milady."

"We'll stay hereabouts," she replied. "I feel safer knowing my own men are around me than in some strange inn with you all in a separate bunk room."

Rob caught Mallock looking at him and nodded to convey his agreement. "I'll move the horses," he said. "They need better grazing. There's another clearing on the far side of the pond. It's not far. Defiant found it."

Mallock nodded back. "We can move the camp closer to the pond and further from the road since there are only four to share the watch instead of eight." He turned to his troopers. "Come on you lot."

Rob stood and stretched, wincing at his aches and pains. Selene got up too. "I will help you."

Rob smiled at Selene's tired expression. "That's a kind offer, milady, but I can see to the horses myself."

"I'm not asking because I think you need the help, Rob," Selene said with a cool glare. "I'm telling you because I can't bear to be idle."

Evening sunlight filtered gold and green through the canopy of breeze-trembled leaves as Rob double and triple checked Defiant's hobble and stroked her neck in praise at her calm acceptance of the restraint. Darkness whinnied once or twice and listened for answers then seemed satisfied when only the remaining Galloway bothered to reply. Captain Mallock shared out provisions then set one man to watch the road until nightfall. The other two troopers gathered wood for a new fire on the excuse that it would bring some warmth and cheer, but Mallock informed them curtly that it was not necessary. Seeing their sullen frowns, Rob piped up, "Captain?"

"Problem with the animals?" Mallock asked, walking over.

"No," Rob said out of earshot of the two troopers, "but I would also like a camp-fire, if you and Lady Selene will allow it. You and your men must have some tall tales worth telling."

Mallock laughed and punched Rob's arm. "The tallest. Very well. I will ask Selene when she returns from bathing and inform the men to choose only stories they'd happily tell their grandmothers."

"Have you met my Gramma?" Rob said with a wink and wide grin. Mallock laughed again and clapped Rob on his shoulder before walking away.

The evening was the most pleasant Rob had spent for as long as he could remember. Mallock and his men seemed at ease with Lady Selene joining them, and Rob supposed that was because they were her guardsmen and not Sir Eric's. Nobody mentioned plans for the next day until Rob brought it up quietly with Selene when Mallock went to take his turn by the road and the three troopers sat a little way off playing cards by firelight. "What will you do?" Rob asked, sitting as close to Selene as he dared.

Selene sighed deeply. "I suppose I should instruct Mallock to pack up camp early, get us back on the road and stop in town to enquire if Eric is recovering. We could find rooms for the night, or we could press on. Eric thought that if we did not stop, from here, one full day would do it. But I would rather take a random road at the next crossroads. I threatened Sir Eric I might, but I believed him when he told me how quickly I'd be found and married off to someone else."

"Ah." Rob let out a deep sigh. "Gramma says running from a problem won't solve it. I can see only one way you might avoid an unwelcome marriage and I doubt you would find it any more palatable."

Selene frowned into the flames and leaned her head on Rob's shoulder. "I will listen to any ideas now, however outrageous."

"Well," Rob said, pulling on his lower lip with his teeth for a few seconds and trying to quell the flutter in his stomach. "You can only be married to one man. So marry one you like. Tomorrow."

Selene sat upright immediately, and Rob's face flared with more than the heat of the fire. He turned to face her with an apology ready on his lips, but froze when he saw not shock or horror, but an enthralled smile. "Rob! I had the same idea. Earlier today, when I stared at him out cold from Defiant's kick. I said nothing then because it wasn't the right time for it. Eric and his men would have stopped me or found me. But he's unable and I've sent his men away." Selene's voice gathered pace as the idea took root and grew branches. "I'd have to bribe a magistrate but that should not be too difficult. Eric has silver stashed in his belongings. I'd need two witnesses, employed men or men of standing." She stopped and took a few breaths to calm herself and leaned against Rob again. "It might work. They say marry in haste then repent at leisure, but I think I know someone who would not break my heart. Rob, stay near me tonight. When Thomas returns from his watch, ask him to wake me."

Rob made the promise with lead in his gut and rock in his chest. The other men gave up their game and sat by the fire for warmth, ate whatever was left over from the evening meal, and settled to sleep.

Selene yawned despite her excitement and retreated into her tent, leaving Rob to watch the fire die down to embers before he traipsed through the moonlight to check where the horses were and freshen up best he could at the pond before wrapping up in his blanket outside Selene's tent and hoping for sleep.

He awoke to quiet voices from inside the tent. "I hope to avoid it by already being married to a good man I know."

Rob's heart almost stopped in his chest. Mallock laughed. "So you have another suitor waiting?"

"I may have," Selene replied. "He is someone I admire."

Rob felt the dull ache of a pointless hope crushed. He blinked away the prickle in his eyelids and breathed deep to ease the weight in his chest.

"Although I am sure we like each other," Selene continued oblivious to the misery only a few feet away, creeping closer to her tent flap, "he's not of noble birth and would not insist that I produce heirs. He is young and handsome and kind. We are not in love, not yet, but we could live happily enough together. Perhaps love will find us in time."

Rob sat up and moved closer to Selene's tent, unable to keep his words contained. "Whoever he is, he is lucky."

Selene moved the canvas flap aside and looked out. She put

her hand out to Rob and waved it, beckoning, until he clasped her fingers. "Rob Kerry," Selene said, squeezing his hand. "Are you an idiot?"

In the morning, Mallock rode into town with one trooper and some silver, tasked with finding a magistrate in need of it. The other two troopers packed up camp. Selene helped Rob with the horses, all the while instructing him to stand straighter, swagger more, and generally do the best he could to look like a nobleman fallen on hard times. She gave him a dress uniform, the jacket with brighter dye and shinier buttons and stripes like Mallock's. "He was to wear it at my wedding, as my witness," Selene said as she helped Rob fasten the jacket. "Is it not odd that I can have two so different cousins? Eric is the proud son of my mother's brother. Thomas is the result of an indiscretion of my father's sister. I'm not supposed to know that, but I used to listen to the servants' gossip when they thought my ears too tender to hear."

"I doubt we'll ever have servants," Rob said drily. "I'm about to lose my job as Sir Eric's hostler so my income is gone."

"I'll see all the men paid up front from his purse and we'll be careful with the remainder," Selene said with a soft laugh. "You'll get by, Rob Kerry, and so will I."

Smartened up as best he could be under the circumstances, Selene fussed with Rob's borrowed belt buckle until she declared it shiny enough. Rob submitted to the attention with a face that flushed with various hues of red and pink and was rewarded with a sparkling grin. "As I said before," Selene observed, "very handsome."

Shortly after midday, Mallock returned and gave the good news that he had found a magistrate willing to overlook the groomsman's exact circumstances and the reading of the banns for a sum that would settle one gambling debt and enable him to accrue another, and he awaited their arrival.

"Let Sprite carry a pack today. I want to see you up on Darkness," Selene said.

Rob adjusted the saddle and hauled himself up onto the Friesian while the beast shifted. The great black head turned, eyes rolling, to try to see exactly what was on his back, then Rob scratched and stroked the beast's thick neck, telling Darkness how good he was in a calm voice. Darkness blew and stamped, ready to be off. Selene laughed. "He suits you," she said. "Shame we have to leave him for Eric."

By the time they had reached town, Rob knew he would be sorry to say goodbye to the powerful Friesian too.

Hours later, safely wed, fed and housed in a modest candlelit room, Rob shook out his breeches and folded them. Something fell, glinted and chinked and rolled. Selene stamped on it before it vanished under the bed and picked it up. "Yours?"

Rob took the object and laughed. "It's a silver coin! When I was a child, I kept a shiny one just like this for luck. I lost it." His brow wrinkled. "No, not lost. Ma and I dropped it down a well and I made three wishes."

Selene's face lit up with delight. "What did you wish for?"

"I can't remember," said Rob. He rubbed at the heads and the tails, feeling the bumps and grooves of the patterned surfaces. "Oh! First, I wished my father would leave."

"And?" asked Selene, leaning forward.

"They said his heart gave out. I helped bury him. My second wish was to be allowed to leave my old life behind, live as who I am, as Robert and not... someone that wasn't me."

"Two out of three," said Selene. "What was your third wish?"

"No." Rob laughed at the warm memory of flashing copper hair, a bright smile and pale skin speckled with freckles, and chanted, "If you tell it breaks the spell!"

"I will make you," threatened Selene with a playful twinkle in her eye. "I promise I can!"

Rob shuffled over beside his wife and leaned close, voice low and serious. "I wished that I would leave service and make a life for myself. A life I could share with someone. Someone who'd love me for who I am."

Selene took Rob's hand and opened it. She lifted the silver coin and held it up to the candlelight.

"Perhaps this wish is what brought you to me." She smiled at Rob. "I am thankful. May I keep it?"

"Of course. I have nothing else to give you."

"Oh?" Selene sat close to Rob on the bed, her hand landing lightly on his bare thigh. "I don't think that's true at all."

"I thought all of this too much to wish for," Rob said. Then he kissed Selene and murmured, "But my ma always said that sometimes we have to make our wishes come true all by ourselves."

AUTHOR BIO

Ali is a science educator by day, a fiction writer by night, and has been an unapologetic daydreamer since birth.

Whilst studying physics at university, Ali chose to interpret the 'scientists can't write' stereotype as a personal challenge and has been writing down their daydreams ever since, with some of those daydreams leading to Ali's triptych of novellas, Chrysalides, here with Improbable Press.

Ali has also written "Dancing in the Shallows" for Improbable Press' anthology Dark Cheer: Cryptids Emerging (Volume Blue), and has an extensive back-catalogue of fanfiction as Rudbeckia on AO3.

Ali can also be found on Twitter @alicoylewrites, and on Wordpress at alicoylewrites.wordpress.com.

AUTHOR ACKNOWLEDGEMENTS

Turning a few loose ideas into stories that other people might want to read is a journey.

I owe thanks to many people for making sure that journey had a destination. I would like to thank Atlin for being a patient tactfully realistic collaborative editor. I would like to thank the team at Improbable Press for making this book exist in real life.

And I would like to thank Sean for always telling me I'm brilliant even when I'm not.

www.ingramcontent.com/pod-product-compliance
Lightning Source LLC
Chambersburg PA
CBHW031311280626
47169CB00018B/1198